Miss Rhode Island

NORMAN KOTKER

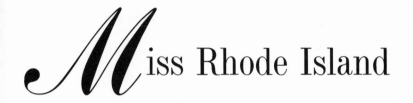

Miss Rhode Island

FARRAR STRAUS GIROUX

New York

Copyright © 1978 by Norman Kotker

All rights reserved

Published simultaneously in Canada by

McGraw-Hill Ryerson Ltd., Toronto

Printed in the United States of America

Designed by Karen Watt

First edition, 1978

Library of Congress Cataloging in Publication Data
Kotker, Norman. / Miss Rhode Island. / I. Title.
PZ4.K8686Mi 1978 [PS3561.0844] 813'.5'4 78–7261

8.24.78 Baker 5.68

for Harry and Betty Kotker

R-3

Miss Rhode Island

I

What is more beautiful, Connecticut or Rhode Island?

Rhode Island, with its misty peninsulas? They arch into the sea, dividing the waves. On Moonstone Beach, the stones glisten. On Mount Hope cherry birches ripple in the wind.

But have you ever seen the shining Housatonic or climbed the leafy hills above the broad Connecticut? Have you ever walked at the end of a summer rain along the silky avenues leading down to the shore at Darien?

Who is more beautiful, the governor or the governor's wife? The Attorney General or the Secretary of State? The president of Brown or the president of Yale? The selectmen of Stonington? The fire department at Narragansett Pier?

Who is more beautiful, your first child or your second?

Who is more beautiful, you or me?

Do you remember how cold you felt the day you looked into the mirror and learned that you weren't beautiful, when you heard the word "beauty"—she's a great beauty, he's incredibly handsome, she's a knockout, he's really something terrific, he turns me on, she's got a great pair of tits, woo-woo. You looked, you got the tape

3

measure, you smiled seductively—do you know how to smile seductively yet?—you hoped, you kneaded, you pushed out, you stretched to make it bigger, pulling on it, and then the next day you were the same; them, they were the beauties, the winners, Adonises. Maybe you could be Most Likely to Succeed, you could entice God, Jesus loved you, but who wanted you most of all?

Not all movie stars are extremely good-looking. Look at Dustin Hoffman, Barbra Streisand. Track practice, football practice, pitching practice, all the 50¢ pieces wasted on the miniature golf course, the quarters thrown away on the pinball machines.

I know all the words in the top ten, plus the words of one of the golden oldies this week, "King of the Road." I know all the state capitals, I can name the six continents, seven: Australia. I wore a bra before she did. I got my period before you did. She's sixteen years old and still hasn't got her period yet. I can run faster than my brother. North Kingstown beat South Kingstown two years in a row in baseball. Connie Mack, the famous baseball personality, got his start right here in the Blackstone Valley League. Nelson Eddy comes from Rhode Island. Van Johnson was born in Newport, now there's someone handsome. Maybe someday I will be handsome too, this is an awkward age, that's what it says in the books. If she says no, I can steal my father's car and run it right off the bridge into the bay, you can do that when you're going sixty, gun it right down to the floor.

When I was eight I knew how to drive a real motorcycle, nobody else can say that, my cousin showed me, he didn't show my brother. As for my brother, I am going to arrange it. Someday he will be killed.

4

Have you ever been to Rhode Island?

If you've been to Rhode Island, you've been to Providence. If you've been to Providence, you've seen the State House—how could you miss it?—and on top of it a big dome, a boobie, enormous, you want to squeeze it, floating there over the middle of town. In Boston the State House dome is only a B cup, maybe just an A. But as for Providence, it's a D; it must be, it's the second-largest unsupported dome in the world.

Twenty miles west of the State House dome, over the trees, thousands of them, elms dying of the blight, maples just ready to bud now in this season, over the hickories, the willows, the cherry birches, over the miscellaneous trees—who can identify them? there are so many of them; they all have different shapes and presences, but they all look alike—it's Connecticut. Ten miles north, you're over the border, zip, into the big time, Massachusetts. Thirty miles south, dunk, into the sea; it's a small state, Little Rhody. And eight miles away, southward, in Warwick, at the Howard Johnson Convention Center, in the red velvet room set up for the receptions of the brides of Rhode Island, for the golden wedding anniversaries, for the annual balls of the St. Jean Baptiste Union of America, Rhode Island Branch, even for the meetings of the NAACP, the room with the flocked wallpaper in a fleur-de-lys pattern, an accidental tribute to the many Rhode Islanders of Franco-American descent, there she is, standing up tall, just look at her, catch it while you can, blond and blue-eyed, the winner, Miss Rhode Island.

Yvonne Doucette.

A winner!

You better believe it.

A real winner, this time no one could doubt it, after

5

all these years. The best winner in history, the best Miss Rhode Island anybody had ever seen and one of the judges had, no lie, been judging the contest for thirty-four years; he was a judge before she was even born, an old experienced judge the year her father and mother, with all their frisky little chromosomes jiggling, spunked out just the right ones, the perfect ones to produce her.

36–24–36. Look at it, a winning combination. Don't think half the judges didn't rush right out that night and put that number down on the nigger pool; and don't think they didn't win. A sure sign. As God is watching over Rhode Island, sending his little white clouds over to bring the rain in its season, sending the wind to blow the sails in the bay out into curves, those voluptuous curves: a winner.

Furthermore, she was a Wellesley girl.

She wasn't a low-class mill girl or a secretary out of Bryant and Stratton; she wasn't a supermarket cashier, though she had put in a summer once behind the counter at Almac's in Wakefield. She was a real live Wellesley girl, nothing but the best.

"What do you plan to be?" one of the judges, Kirby, the television personality from Boston, asked her. The answer was already there on her questionnaire sitting Xeroxed right in front of him.

She smiled, authentically—there was no question about it; a high score on poise—and answered without hesitation: "A Latin teacher." At the L her pink tongue lapped at the air for a second, the air he was breathing; at the R, briefly, her moist and glossy lips seemed almost to pucker. "I'll have to teach in a college because"—a little Marilyn Monroe pause, a sob of breath—"the schools aren't teaching it much anymore."

6

Amo, amas, amat. Wiggily-o, wiggily-ass, wiggily-at. Cunnus, custis, cunt. That's not exactly what you'd call a dying language!

As she first walked down the runway, back and forth in a sea-blue bikini, remarkably both tucked in and nearly overflowing, almost falling out—pivoting carefully on her toes as she had been taught to do in high school during drill class—the contingent from North Kingstown shouted joyously for her and the people from South Kingstown, and even some from Warwick although there was a Miss Warwick competing. But she was known in Warwick, she had dated there, she had gone to proms in Warwick. And even people from Providence cheered, from Woonsocket, from Pawtucket, because she was one of the two girls there with a French name. Later when they put the crown on her head—made by Gorham of Providence, silver plate on a special lightweight base— she didn't cry, her lips didn't quiver. She unfocused her eyes a little to block out the view of the audience below to substitute the view of the ocean she could see out of her bedroom window. Ocean, she heard the applause, the Ocean State.

On the way back down the runway at the end of the victory walk she kept her pace steady by sermonizing: Skin Deep. The Eye of the Beholder.

Her speech: "I want to thank everyone for the confidence that has been accorded to me. And I deeply appreciate your choosing me. This is an outstanding day in my life." She could already feel a subtle pressure on her head from the weight of the glistening crown. She had to stiffen her shoulders a little bit to balance it. Naturally that made her figure stand out better. "And I want to say I'll do my best to live up to your expectations. Thank you very much."

7

Such applause! Perhaps she should be a politician, not a Latin teacher.

"And there's one more thing I want to say." Though the applause hadn't died down completely. "I think all the other girls up here on stage ought to share in the honor just as much."

Not in the script. Was she a Communist? There was a sudden silence in the auditorium. Was she alternate culture? Maybe she was lib.

"Because I really didn't expect to win."

It was so quiet she could hear echoes.

"And I have to say it, I don't feel better than the other girls. I don't want you to think I feel superior." Here the lip quivered, the eyes began to fill with tears. A real beauty queen! "It's just a matter of chance, And I think you ought to applaud every single one of the other girls just as much.

"And I insist on it."

The queen was speaking.

Loud applause.

The contestant who came in second, Nelda Mack, Miss Black Is Beautiful, did she see this for what it was: racist? If number one was going to give it away, it ought to go to the runner-up, not to the duds, right?

Miss Pawtucket, not in the running, did she see this right away for what it was? No Miss Rhode Island had ever won in Atlantic City. This one would never be Miss America either; ergo, she was already running for Miss Congeniality instead, right?

Miss Pawtucket, Miss Woonsocket, Miss Westerly, Miss Providence, Miss Rhode Island Italo-American War Veterans, Miss Black Is Beautiful, Miss Knights of Columbus. Yvonne watched them all parading down the runway, one more time, to halfhearted applause.

8

It was her suggestion. It was her victory.

And up above in the heavens, the goddess Pulchritudo gazed down at the losers walking forlornly forward and back along the runway. Their last trip down. Now all they had to look forward to was the church aisle and the path of years. The future was already over. Pawtucket's ankles wobbled. Woonsocket's shoulders sagged. Westerly, a dangerous Irish girl with freckles, a real competitor, forgot to smile; she looked angry. Miss Congeniality, my ass!

Yvonne sat on her throne holding her bouquet of white roses. The auditorium had only two spotlights. Neither one was on her. For the first time, with great interest, she began to inspect the different girls she had defeated.

Sitting in the dark for any length of time is depersonalizing; psychological studies have shown it, with strange noises, applause, calls, obscene shouts assaulting through the darkness like bad thoughts. The subjects studied often seek solace by clutching or fondling their genital zones, not something Yvonne could or would consider doing, even on impulse, at a time like this or in a place like this. "Is that my own girl up there? I don't believe it." Magically out of all that noise, over the oceanic sound, her mother's voice floated—Charlotte Arnold (of the Rhode Island Arnolds) Doucette, sitting down there in the darkness among the Rhode Islanders. "Is that my little girl?" A good question. Fino, Poulos, Kirby: in all that wet-mouthed crowd, there was not one man out there who had ever touched Yvonne disrespectfully, though she had once heard with a surprising thrill that her father often had changed her diapers. She didn't need to touch herself as a reminder of who she was in the

9

darkness, the darkness Poulos had loved; it meant he could touch her where he wanted, if she wanted him to.

The spotlight found Miss Rhode Island already smiling. Sitting composedly on her gilded chair, not exactly a throne, but at least a Louis Quinze. The arms and legs gently curved. The seat perfectly padded. Forward and back, forward and back, the light played on her like the waves of the sea, like time, like years, suns, days passing over Rhode Island. She was supposed to sit there while the people applauded. Then they would hand her a check and her cup—a trophy, as if she had bowled them over, right down the alley, with all the duckpins falling, tumbling over time after time.

In the family section right next to the runway, surrounded by the Coughlins of Westerly, the surly Viggios from East Providence, numerous Perraults from Woonsocket, the da Monizes, all of them small, all of them uneducated, from Central Falls, they sat, the winning family: Doucette.

"I don't believe it." Charlotte's voice. "I don't believe it, I'd like to go right up there and hold her on my lap."

Twenty-five hundred dollars in scholarship money had been donated by the Rhode Island Chamber of Commerce. Now they were a family that owned a color TV and a new portable hair dryer, a stereo and fifty dollars' worth of records or tapes, a lifetime pass to the Imperial Theatre in Providence. And it had all begun as a practical joke.

Time for the queen's parents to be brought up on stage. Her father put his arm around her nervously. He dared do it: a kiss. Her mother giggled. "Congratulations," she said. It had been Joseph's practical joke. Horny brother Joseph and Emilie, Yvonne's little sister. Now, ha-ha, the joke was on them.

10

All the men who had ever kissed Yvonne or felt her up would have pushed harder if they'd known at the time they were grabbing at a beauty queen. There's no denying that. Therefore she had to watch out. That's what her mother warned her and her father too, the next morning at breakfast. "They're all going to be after you now."

But was that really true?

Kirby, Poulos, even Fino. Not one of them called.

Her brother Joseph danced attendance at the breakfast table, though.

"Pass me an orange," Yvonne asked her father.

But it was Joseph who picked one up and tossed it to her. Too fast, rough, abrupt. She was lucky to catch it.

"That's no way to treat the beauty queen," Doucette said indignantly. "Watch out, now." It had been five years since he had last hit Joseph.

Yvonne swiveled in her chair, she reached out to the sideboard, she pulled open the drawer to get a sharp knife. Peeling the orange without it could break a fingernail. Her left breast pushed through a space in the chair back, as if the designer, Chippendale himself, had known she was coming along. "I'm going to take a nap this afternoon. I'll just be lazy." Her voice expanded with pleasure. "After all, I'm the queen. Maybe I'll just get into the car and go down to some beach." She stuck the point of the knife into her orange.

"You have to stay here." Charlotte leaned forward and grabbed an orange too. "People come by, you want to say hello. You just had your hair set. It's too cold to go to the beach yet."

"But I'm going out." Joseph the teaser! He had been admitted to Brown, he had his own car, he had earned the money for it. What reason did he have to stay home!

"You got me into this." Yvonne's sharp knife twisted

11

around and around. "You should stay home and take the consequences too."

"I'll stay home with you in the morning, but not this afternoon." Joseph made it sound as though he were actually giving something up. Their parents and Emilie were going to church. That left the two of them alone in the house, walking past each other from room to room.

She read the newspaper in her bedroom. He shaved in the bathroom. She washed the breakfast dishes in the kitchen. In the dining room he started on the Sunday crossword puzzle.

"What's a four-letter word meaning desire?"

"I know, but I wouldn't tell you." A quick, decisive twist and she shut the kitchen faucet off tight.

He went out into the yard to set up the lawn sprinkler. She went up into her room and closed the door, to try on her bathing suit one more time. She stood in front of the mirror, facing front, then pivoted around in profile, holding in the little belly curve, but not too much. He watched the spout of the lawn hose turning this way and that for a minute or two. It got warm on the lawn; he took off his shirt. She went into the bathroom and took a shower. She rubbed her body dry with a big red towel, she patted herself between the legs with it. She raised her arms and rolled deodorant onto the armpits, and then held her arms up in the air until it dried. She stood in front of her mirror and brushed her hair, stroke after stroke, stroke after stroke, until their parents came home from church.

In the evening her roommate Julie called up, long-distance from Wellesley. "What does it feel like?" Repeated three times. Each time it sounded like a squeal.

"It doesn't feel like anything, not a damn thing."

"I can't imagine it, it has to feel like something. What

12

are you clamming up for? Is someone in the room with you?"

"No, I'm down in the playroom."

"Is someone listening in on the extension?"

Yvonne's sister was out of the house.

"Come off it, Yvonne. Don't queens talk?"

"O.K., I'll tell you." Her parents and Joseph were sitting outside on the porch. "You hear noises, all the cars going by, the boys shouting it out, I don't know what; that's what I heard all last night. They were honking horns, they must have driven over from everywhere, Fall River, Providence, I don't know how they found me, but you couldn't stop them, it went on all night. Up and down, up and down, gunning it, and everything they said —you should hear it—eat it, eat it, stuff like that, vroom, vroom, vroom, come on out, let's fuck, I swear it."

"Jesus, why didn't you call the police?"

Yvonne held the receiver against her cheek for a minute. "I couldn't, how could I, I thought I was cracking. Maybe I was just imagining it, and when I came downstairs this morning I said to my mother, 'Did you hear that, last night, all that noise?' She didn't say anything, she just gave me this blank look and said, 'No, maybe it was Joseph snoring.'"

"And when do you get your prizes?" Julie's voice turned noncommittal.

"I don't know, I don't care about the prizes, what does it matter to me, I'm sorry I even did it. All night. They go riding back and forth in front of the house all night like in a movie and all I want to do is get out of here and go off somewhere, out of Wickford, not back to Wellesley but someplace brand-new, everybody looks at me creepy, nobody wants to touch me."

Julie began to laugh. "You're making a joke."

13

"I mean it. Nobody's called me, I've been home all day, it's eight o'clock, nobody called. Just the woman from the committee, she had to, it was official. The woman from across the street came over too, she brought a pie, she thought it would come in handy, we'd have company. She was wrong, nobody came. She just talked to my mother, she didn't even see me, she was in and out of the house before I even came into the room."

"She was shy in front of you."

"Why?" Yvonne could feel the tears forming in the space behind her eyes, that hidden place. To stop them she pressed her thumb against her forehead, leaving a red mark.

"The man next door was working on his garden, I went out on the porch. You know what he said? He said, 'Hi, how's it going, Yvonne.' That's what he said."

"People think you're busy."

"I'm not busy."

"Maybe you're tired. People are going to hold back. I held back before I called you. I waited, people are going to wait."

"Why?"

On the queen's forehead, the red mark slowly faded away. "Nobody has to treat me any different. It was all supposed to be a joke. But I never thought it was funny."

A joke.

In the summer there had been signs in store windows all over town.

TRICENTENNIAL QUEEN
Single girls only
Prizes
Pick up application here

As a joke, her brother Joseph and her little sister had filled out a questionnaire, forged her signature on it, and dropped it off at the drugstore.

"What interview?" Yvonne had said when the committee called her.

"For the Tricentennial beauty queen."

"Oh," Yvonne said quietly. "Oh my." She was alone in the room when the call came, but she began to blush anyway.

Just what the song says: Flattery can charge your battery.

"That's very kind of you," she said. The voice of a proper Wellesley girl.

The town calls, you answer. You have no choice. The goddess hovering over the earth will tell you, you have no choice. You get into the car and drive, thighs resting lightly on the edge of the car seat, soft feet pumping the accelerator, white palms warm on the steering wheel. Clothes: low heels, a skirt of middle length. Makeup: lightish.

"How do you like North Kingstown as compared to Wellesley? Do you expect to come back to Rhode Island after you finish college, it's so small here? Do you have a special boyfriend?"

"I like it here best. Oh, I hope so." Rhode Island, small as a child, could anyone desert it! "No, there's nobody special."

It wasn't until the interview was almost over and the doorbell rang and another girl came in that Yvonne realized it: It wasn't a coronation, it was a contest.

But then it was too late for her to back out. So what! Two years running in high school she had been voted Most Beautiful. She had also been voted Most Likely to Succeed.

15

Eight girls had pictures up on the town bulletin board on the little green next to the bridge. Beneath each picture was a name and a little plastic bank so voters could drop pennies in. The girl with the most pennies would win.

$1.39 could win it. $1.54. There were only 16,000 people in town. $160 worth of pennies would make it unanimous.

"I screwed this pussy," someone wrote with Magic Marker under the picture of one of the girls. The girl's father left work when he was told about it and came down to the center of town with adhesive tape to cover up the words. Joseph was full of regret when he heard about it. He got a roll of fifty dimes and put them into the bank under his sister's picture. Only pennies counted, it said. But he did it anyway. Recompense.

"Lovely, lovely, I'm honored, thank you, I appreciate it," Yvonne said when he told her. "You should have taken the money and bought a subscription to *Playboy.*" She was sitting at the piano. She leaned forward slightly over the white keys, her arms stretched out sheltering her breasts. Without waiting for an answer, she began playing again.

Joseph stood over her, he put his hand lightly on her shoulder, he tried to make her turn around. "Take it as a compliment. Sit back and enjoy it."

But she wouldn't look him in the eyes.

Especially when she won.

$3.84. 63¢ ahead of the runner-up.

Wearing a tinsel crown bought with the proceeds of the contest, she handed out the prizes in the potato-sack races. She gave one cup to the winner of the sailboat race, another to the winner of the tuna derby. Miss North Kingstown. If she didn't compete for the title of Miss

Rhode Island, she could never show her face in town again. That face, that face, that beautiful face, as they sing every year on TV during the Miss America contest. Those blue eyes. That victorious smile. That perfect chin where someday, she expected, a mole would grow, just as it grew on her mother's chin.

Her majesty, Yvonne I, queen of Rhode Island, dressed in a pink flowered nightgown, high-necked, puff sleeves, lay on her bed. Behind her head was a maple headboard; beyond her feet a footboard, smaller, maple too. At her left, across the green rug, a maple chest of drawers. Above it in the darkness, a mirror. The wood frame had once been tree; the glass, sand. Yvonne faced north. One window was at her right hand, one at her feet. In her nightgown, on her bed, on a platform of wood, braced and set on earth, in Wickford in North Kingstown, Rhode Island, the smallest United State.

The queen of Massachusetts slept in a room in Lynn; the queen of Nebraska slept in her boxlike room in Hastings; the queen of Indiana in Indianapolis—all of them breathing up and down like the sea.

North America floats on its plate of stone over the fire in the core of the earth. The earth turns around the sun, creating time. Molten rock spills up out of the ocean floor east of Narragansett Bay, creating time. Venus tilts in the heavens. The blond hairs grow by micromillimeters along the nape of the neck of the queen of Rhode Island, under her arms, creating time. Her reign is 1/365 over.

In the next room her sister is breathing; though the sea air comes in the window, tonight she is almost gasping, it is difficult for her to breathe. Down the hall, her brother lies dreaming of the queens, the queen of Nebraska, the queen of Africa, the princesses of Portugal, those he sees every day walking disdainfully in the streets of Providence. He rolls over; his hand is between his legs.

Her mother and her father lie in their bed not touching. Her father moves his leg and feels the warmth of his wife's foot. As if it were stone, not warm flesh, he moves his leg away fast. Often they touch in bed; usually they lie together. But tonight, like last night, unaccountably the dowager and the father of the queen—they are not touching.

II

I win, you lose. I'm the cowboy, you're the Indian. I'm the Yankees, you're the Red Sox. Or even worse.

Deeanne Connell told me she was going to vote for me, she said, "I think you're going to win it for best-looking; Alicia, she doesn't stand a chance. I know how the voting's going to go, everybody in the class knows."

Frankly, I would just as soon not vote, I think these contests are awful. But I voted because I think Shooter is the best athlete; he was all-conference, he was all-state, he was all-New England, and I think the whole school should get behind him.

I marked my ballot: North Kingstown sucks.

I wrote my own name in for everything: handsomest, prettiest, best athlete, boys and girls. Most talented. You should see me do the Latin Hustle. You should see me shake the baton. Drill team, that's my talent.

What is a good Ivy League talent anyway?

Show jumping?

Yvonne had been on a horse only once.

Flute playing. That was too suggestive-looking for a beauty queen.

Piano? But she could never play three minutes on stage without a mistake. Could you? Then don't judge, don't sit there laughing at them in the dark in your living room while the TV set is glowing in its dim colors. Beethoven, Minuet in G, *A Treasury of Easy Classics,* page eighteen, four mistakes. That was good enough for the Miss Rhode Island contest. But for Miss America there were no mistakes allowed.

An Ivy League talent: splitting the atom, field hockey. Neither one of them a solo. A Southern or Western talent: baton twirling, acrobatic dancing, playing the harmonica, drumming, playing the trumpet, the accordion, singing "Summertime" by George Gershwin. A Wellesley talent: aria singing, ballet possibly, definitely modern dance. Could a girl perfect, or even learn modern dance well enough to enter the Miss America contest with it? And then improve enough between April and Labor Day weekend to be able to compete? Even an athletic girl, an admittedly graceful girl?

Figure skating? The famous Tenley Albright—Radcliffe. The Olympic champion Dick Button—Harvard. When she was little, Yvonne already knew how to do a figure 8. She could skate on one leg and hold the other behind her. She could turn ten, maybe twelve times, and fast too—actually spin, an authentic spin. After she went to Providence one Saturday night with her parents and brother, up and around long dizzying stairways to seats overlooking the Ice Capades, she taught herself to lean forward and spread her arms out while skating, even to do a little tiptoe work. She could skate backwards, dancing, if someone supported her. She had skated every winter on the pond behind the cemetery, dodging out of the way of the boys who played hockey. She was a French Canadian. There was a myth in her family—her father maintained it—they were distantly related to Maurice the Rocket Richard.

Skating—that was her talent.

The Ice Capades spend the summer in Atlantic City training. They vacate Convention Hall the Friday before Labor Day to make way for the Miss America Pageant. "Sure they can get ice in there," Mrs. Melli, the Rhode Island pageant organizer, said, Mrs. Melli who would be her chaperone in Atlantic City. "Don't worry." Every year they sent Mrs. Melli a list of acceptable talents. Figure skating was on the list.

There was an arena in Cranston. There was one in North Providence. But they had one bad aspect: Figure skating is not a talent a girl can practice in private. In Cranston, a short woman with brass-blond hair and a shining white satin skirt, the manager, skated over the weekend after Yvonne was crowned Miss Rhode Island. "I saw your picture in the paper. Congratulations," she said. "That's wonderful. Do you want to take lessons?" Yvonne practiced her spin, conservatively, did one or two forward glides with her arms spread on either side, first with the left leg held back and then with the right. The loudspeaker was playing a medley from *Oklahoma!* "Pretty good," the woman said to her unpleasantly. "But you could use some improvement in your form."

And in the rink in North Providence, little boys, a troop of Cub Scouts in uniform, giggled and nudged each other and tumbled down onto the ice in excitement when she raised one leg and glided forward toward them, her arms spread, her breasts hanging down inside her ribbed knit sweater just at a level with their mouths.

Ice Princess.

The Child of the Canadian North. Miss North America.

At Brine's in Boston: one outfit in white satin with a flared skirt; the same in neon green; also in her size, nine,

21

an ice-blue with sequins sewn on it. Purchased. But for practice only. For Miss America all the ice-skating costumes looked cheap.

The answer: a white body suit with white fake fur sewn around the collar.

"At least your talent is something we don't have to be ashamed of," her mother said. In the evening light in the dining room you could hardly see the mole on her chin. "Not that we would ever be ashamed of anything you did. You or your sister or your brother." But where can you buy fake fur in Rhode Island?

White tulle was available, though. It was easier for her mother to sew, less obvious, icier-looking.

"Why don't you come home again from Wellesley sometime next month so I can try the costume on you. We'll go skating together. I could help you on your routine."

"Mail it up to me," Yvonne said quickly. "I have exams. I'll try it on there."

But there were other, better invitations.

1. To appear on a TV talk show, "Kirby at Midnight." Kirby had been one of the judges and two weeks after the Miss Rhode contest he finally called.

2. Sea Village in Bristol. The best retirement condominium in Rhode Island. Cut the ribbon at the opening. $100. A Saturday afternoon in June.

3. Jordan Marsh at Warwick Mall, the Friday before Easter. Autographing sales slips. Meet Miss Rhode Island. A full-page picture in the *Journal* and the *Evening Bulletin*. $200 in cash or, optional, $200 in merchandise.

4. Queen of the Annual Ball, Quisset Club, Narragansett. The third Saturday night in March. A social distinction. The first Miss Rhode Island in history ever to be invited.

22

5. Queen of the Freshman Dance at Brown. Through Joseph. Turned down.

6. The annual Hasty Pudding Show at Harvard. A walk-on part. Turned down.

7. Hello, I was given your name by Peter Johnson, he thought we should get together and I get out to Wellesley every once in a while from MIT, why don't we get together sometime when I'm out there.

"Who's Peter Johnson?"

"You know, from Cambridge."

A name that sounds familiar. But had she ever met him? A put-on? Warwick High? Turned down.

One week invitations came every single day, even Sunday, not counting kook calls, not counting boys who called for dates, not counting the construction men on Route 16 who cried out at her in agony or groaned as if suffering from her beauty as she walked by.

"I'm tired of answering the phone for you," her roommate Julie said, smiling. "All the girls on the second floor are tired of it."

"Tell them just to let the phone ring. If they want me enough, they'll call back."

"That's just more rings then," Julie said humorlessly.

Still, Julie promised to stay up late to watch her on "Kirby at Midnight." One TV set in Pomeroy Hall. One TV set and thirty-two girls in front of it.

On the show: all six New England beauty queens.

"I don't feel worried that I'll make some awful mistake," Yvonne said to Miss Connecticut before the show. "I don't feel nervous." A TV performer, cool, even though she had never been on TV before. No one could see that inside Yvonne's shoes, her toenails were painted with the same polish as her fingernails, a blushing color, vaginal, a hectic pink. "I don't have any funny feelings in

23

my stomach. I keep saying to myself it doesn't faze me."

"I'm not nervous either." Miss Connecticut, could she be telling the truth? Her curly hair was a little bit out of control.

"But then I say to myself, come off it, Doucette, who are you kidding? You must be nervous, going on TV, what if I fall off my chair? I bet even Kirby's nervous; he seems cool, that could be fake. I've met him, I can tell he's nervous. He jokes too much."

"How'd you meet him?" A sudden cold front. Weather over Connecticut, cloudy, possible storms.

"He was one of my judges. What a job! Decide which one has the best pair."

"He must have voted for you."

"Because I'm majoring in Latin. I think that got him. I recited something by heart. Cicero. You know Cicero, the Roman author. They liked that."

There was a mocking look in Miss Connecticut's dark eyes. "J'étudie le français," she said.

"Oh, that's nice." Yvonne was sincere. "I'm part French."

Miss Connecticut smiled at Yvonne glassily; she had large, perfect teeth, perhaps a little too large. She breathed in so that her bosom showed better. "And I ski too," she said almost as if Yvonne were a judge. "I love to ski, my home town has a ski area, Tapawingo. Have you ever been there? I just love to ski. Do you?" she asked, suddenly cautious.

"I skate, I never skied, I'm too busy skating."

"You ought to try it."

Yvonne tucked her legs beneath her chair a little. Sometimes she was afraid practice could make them too muscular. "Skating is my talent."

24

"I'm a singer," Miss Connecticut said. "Scat," she added triumphantly.

"Scat, yourself!" A strange competitive girl—but pretty!

Miss Connecticut laughed as if she had scored a point.

Could anyone looking at the TV screen tell that they didn't feel friendly to each other? They put their hands on each other's arms, they smiled broadly, when they interrupted it seemed like excitement and not rudeness; there they were, happy girls—all of them, Miss Everything in New England. Miss Maine, how about her? Quite possible, if they wanted a new image this year, with her high wedge shoes and her '30s imitation print dress. Her mouth was small and her lipstick was bright red and heavy. She had a definite look. Miss New Hampshire, outdoorsy, I'm studying to be a veterinarian. Miss Vermont: "If I hadn't won, I'd be married by now. The reason we're holding off is until after the pageant."

"And then you might have to control yourselves for another year." From Kirby this was a dirty joke.

On color TV Miss Vermont blushed. All the other girls laughed. Except for Miss Massachusetts. She adopted an impassive look. Why? Because she had forgotten she was chewing gum until they were already on the air; she had to keep her face immobile. It made her more beautiful. During the first commercial she put the gum into a piece of Kleenex. Then she could smile. Her smile wasn't her best feature, though; it was too wide.

"And what about you?" Kirby turned toward Yvonne and the camera followed, caught her in its circle, she existed within it, in the air, ethereal creature, there were thousands of her all over New England, Miss Air, Miss Everywhere. "Do you think you'll win?"

Yvonne's smile was measured. It flickered a moment like the moon. "I'm going to try my best." The appropriate response, but it didn't answer the question.

"How about the finals, do you think you'll reach the finals?"

There were thousands of Yvonnes, thousands of answers. The philosophy majors will tell you: All the Rhode Islanders see the same moon in the sky, but all the Rhode Islanders see different moons too.

"Let's leave that one up to the judges."

"One more question, Miss Rhode Island. What are you doing right after the show?"

A proposition! Right on TV. From Miss Connecticut all she got for protection was a quick unrevealing smile.

"I'm going back to school, it's late." Stern as a housemother. "After all, I've got to get my beauty sleep."

"Then I'll drive you back."

More like Bobby than Jack, smaller than Teddy, Kirby was good-looking. An Irish cute boy, freckles on his nose. "You folks watching may not know it, but Yvonne here, Miss Rhode Island, is, believe it or not, a Wellesley girl."

Video: Yvonne's pale face.

Audio: Kirby's low rushing voice. He was aggressive, he might have the capacity to go national. Maybe in a few years he'll take over one of the major talk shows.

"It's a long ride back to Wellesley, you shouldn't be out alone late at night, even in a taxi, it's not safe. Besides, I always wanted to see Wellesley by moonlight."

"Even on a night when there's no moon?"

Personality and wit: Miss Rhode Island, nine out of a possible ten.

But the next week when Kirby took her to the opening

of an Andy Warhol show at the Institute of Contemporary Art, he gave most of his attention to Andy Warhol and to a girl wearing a necklace made out of Christmas-tree balls. The silverplate tiara, the red sash with gold-flecked letters—Yvonne's own glitter, that was stored in see-through plastic boxes on a closet shelf, beside her Most Likely to Succeed plaque, her Most Beautiful Senior trophy. Maybe she made the guests nervous. Too beautiful, too straight. The only man who talked to her was a reporter for the Harvard *Crimson*. "What a gathering!" he said happily. "Did you come up from New York?"

"Oh no." The mistake startled Yvonne. "I've only been to New York once."

"My God, where do you come from?"

"Rhode Island."

He gave her a funny look and moved away.

No matter. If she wanted Harvard, she could have Fino. He took her out to parties in Cambridge. He was careful to introduce her only by name. Still, they all knew who she was, Miss Rhode Island—the law students and their dates, the graduate students, the young men beginning to teach in Roxbury or work at urban renewal in the mayor of Boston's office. Fino had passed the word around the Law School beforehand. Foxy Fino.

The more daring guests would walk up to her, hiding their nervousness, coming on strong. "How'd you get the name Yvonne?" they'd say. "I never met a Yvonne before. Or is it an Yvonne?"

They were too shy to ask: How'd you get to be a beauty queen? How did you become beautiful? What do you know that you can tell me? Will you let me touch?

"After the five quintuplets," Yvonne would answer smoothly. "My mother was always jealous of them." Emi-

27

lie, Marie, Annette, Cecile, Yvonne. Fame is the spur. "Besides, my father's French Canadian."

"One of you equals five of them," they'd say, or "I always liked French girls." And then they would watch apelike while she danced with Fino, a man taller than they were and still fine-boned.

Those fast jiggles. That swerve. Those flashing hands.

Fino and Kirby—both of them reached for her breasts. Kirby went after her with his mouth too. They both tried to maneuver themselves on top of her, grunting. Fino wrinkling his beautifully fitted trousers. But by the third date, Kirby spoke up. "Hi ho, hi ho, it's into bed we go."

"Well I don't feel quite ready for that." Sitting opposite him on the floor, in a Japanese restaurant, Yvonne folded her hands. "I don't want to hurry everything in my life."

"You want to wait until you get married?"

"Oh, I don't intend to get married for a long time."

"You want to wait for Christmas? You can't do it with Santa Claus. Do you believe in Santa Claus?"

That one she didn't answer.

So what if Kirby had the impression she was the only girl at Wellesley who never smoked grass. Who never put out, a virgin. The only girl at Wellesley who never did it, the only beauty queen.

Fino was smarter. He never asked. He just kept trying.

"You're very hard to pin down since you got to be the queen." It wasn't Fino who said it, it was Julie. "As if you're not there sometimes. You ought to think about that. Maybe your friends are noticing it too."

This time Julie was resentful because Yvonne had no time to go to a Pomeroy House social. Julie was going. Marilyn in the next room was going. They were all going.

"I've got too many things to do. I have to ride the bus every day for an hour just to go ice skating. I've got to do translations. Latin takes time, don't think it's easy."

"You could still spare some time for the house. People will think you're a snob."

"I don't give a damn what they think! Have you ever tried translating Latin poetry? It uses up a lot of time. If I do go down there, it won't be till I finish my work."

> *Montium custos nemorumque, Virgo,*
> *quae laborantis utero puellas*
> *ter vocata audis adimisque leto,*
> *diva triformis,*
>
> *Imminens villae tua pinus esto*
> *quam per exactos ego laetus annos*
> *verris obliquum medantantis ictum*
> *sanguine donem.*

Virgin Goddess (Athena? Diana?) who guards, who watches over the mountains and the woods, when girls in labor of the uterus, in childbirth, call out three times, who listens (to them) and saves (them?), delivers from death, leto? destruction? Three-formed goddess. Mother? Lover? Destroyer?

From now on beside my house this pine tree will be yours which, where for sacrifice I at the beginning of the year will give it the blood of a wild pig. A young wild pig? Aiming its first shaft up? Obliquely?

Because Yvonne's room was right over the Pomeroy parlor, she could hear dimly the sounds of a crowd below.

If you did have to go to one of the dances, it was good to be late.

Downstairs Julie would be fighting her greatest desire:

29

to eat one of the little cakes. She had wanted to bake cookies in the house kitchen. "That's not lib," Yvonne said. But now, when Yvonne got downstairs, she reassured Julie. "You were right, it would have been nice to have cookies too."

With her soft skirt slowly moving back and forth invitingly because, occasionally, she tapped her foot, she stood next to Julie. And next to the boy Julie was talking to. The room was pale, the rug was pale, the sofa fabric subdued, the walls a quiet color. None of the dresses were a bright pink.

"I hate these dances. I don't know why I come or make a fuss about them." Julie had admitted it, she was behind in Psychology of the Adolescent, she was behind in Sociology 204—American Values. "But it's nice to meet people."

The boy she had found stood between her and Yvonne, turning first to one, then to the other. Attractive, from Pennsylvania, with a tough bristly blond beard. "It's good to get away from books into the real world." He smiled enthusiastically. At which one of them, Yvonne or Julie?

At the edge of the room the spirit of ugliness hovered, near the wide door that led into the hallway. Three girls, all with long hanging hair, thin fingers. Yvonne shivered. All three of them were looking at her. She turned away to face the other direction. Did the boy with the beard think he was being rejected? Was Julie grateful? But another boy, the one over there, the one with pure-blond hair, as blond as hers, silver almost, a Swede, a Finn, he could see it as an invitation; or the one sitting on the sofa with her friend Marilyn, the boy with dark curly hair and long thick legs, a football player.

The next morning she found a movie magazine in the hallway outside her door.

Was it an accident? Had someone dropped it? Was it left there by mistake?

Who at Wellesley would carry around a movie magazine anyway?

But then, the next day when she opened the door to her room, she found another one.

Someone was putting them there.

All that week. There was one every day. A different one too.

One time the magazine was even pushed under the door. It was no accident.

Someone was putting them there.

Every morning, no matter what time she woke up, even on the day she set her alarm clock for six, even when she tried to stay awake in bed all night to listen, no matter whether she opened the door first or Julie did, it was lying there. On the cover, a beautiful face staring upward, waiting for her to step on it as she walked out.

After the third magazine, she started to cry as soon as Julie walked out of the room in the morning. She covered her mouth with a pillow so no one could hear.

But she was tempted to read the magazines too.

Not the first one. That had an article about Tricia Nixon. It went into the wastebasket.

But the second one had a six-page feature on Jackie Kennedy.

That one she read.

The third one had a story about a new French star; it was called "La Sexe Goddess." That she read too.

"Don't worry about it." Julie had a sense of humor. She even clipped out an acne ad from one of the magazines and taped it onto Yvonne's mirror. "Don't let it bother you, it's some senior, she's never been screwed. It's her perversion, that's how she's working it out."

Maybe Julie knew who was doing it.

It was like the beginning of a murder. There could be a knife out there one day. A severed breast. A picture of Ophelia floating face down on the waters and underneath the picture, a caption—one word: Whore. Or a portrait of Philomel, the beautiful raped one, her tongue torn out so she could never tell who it was who had violated her.

"Why should you be concerned about it, Julie? It's not aimed at you."

But then the next morning, there was something else: a bunny, a pinup out of *Playboy* or *Penthouse*, kneeling in the snow, holding up her big pink breasts with her hands. "After her sauna and a romp in the snow, Suzi hugs herself to warm up. There's lots of guys who would be happy to help," it said under the picture.

"I'm going to catch the bitch who's doing this," Yvonne said when she saw it. "I'm going to stay up and catch her and report her. I'm going to ruin her. She'll be expelled out of Wellesley. Do you suppose it's Marilyn, it couldn't be."

"Of course it's not Marilyn!" Julie didn't even look at the pinup. "Don't be ridiculous."

"It makes me nervous. What'll I say to her when I pull the door open? 'There she is, you crazy bitch!' I'll scream it. In the middle of the night, everyone will come running. It has to be somebody from Pomeroy. I'd recognize anybody in the house. I'll hit her, I'll get her face. I'd like to do it."

"Be careful you don't break a fingernail."

"Oh, come off it!" Yvonne held the picture up in front

of her. She waved it in the air to make Julie look. "Do you think this is fun for me? Any girl who's doing it has to be jealous, I don't like to say it. I don't like to blow my own horn. But why else would anyone do something stupid like this?"

"Maybe they don't approve of beauty contests. Maybe it's one of the lib people."

Maybe it was Julie, but how could she manage it unless she got up in the middle of the night and pretended to slip the magazine under the door?

"Maybe it's some secret dikes, I wouldn't be surprised. They hate normal sex."

"That's a terrible thing to say." Julie's answer was quick as a slap. Yvonne had forgotten. Julie was a dues-paying member of the Civil Liberties Union. "They have a right. You should be ashamed to think like that. You're getting hysterical about it."

"I don't give a damn if I get hysterical, it's a lot of pressure. You don't know the pressure, it doesn't matter to you. What's it to them? Why should they care who has the prettiest ass in Rhode Island?" Angrily, Yvonne twisted the dial of her alarm clock to make it ring at 12:30. "I'm going to sleep early tonight. You better wake me up when you go to bed."

But that night when the alarm clock rang at 12:30, all the lights were out and Julie, startled out of sleep, was calling out hoarsely, "Shut it off! Shut it off!"

"It serves you right for not waking me up when I asked you to." Yvonne took her time shutting the alarm clock off.

She pulled the electric blanket off her bed. She found a socket to plug it into. She wrapped herself in the blanket and settled down next to the door, making certain that she sat touching the threshold. If she fell asleep, a

33

paper pushed under the door would wake her up, it would hit up against her.

Encountering the most beautiful ass in Rhode Island. The truth is the truth.

Certainly the most beautiful at Wellesley.

Perhaps the most beautiful in America.

The shade was drawn. Yvonne got up to raise it. That way a little light would come into the room. But when she was seated again inside her blanket, the room was still black with night. Psychological studies have shown it: Sitting in the dark for any length of time is depersonalizing. The subjects studied often seek solace by fondling their genital zones. After searching the darkness for any sign of light, their eyes close. But their ears remain acutely sensitive, listening for any sound. After a while, though, they tune sound out too.

When Yvonne woke up suddenly, with the sun on her face, she knew she hadn't just dreamed it: there was another dirty picture alongside her in the room. Without opening her eyes, she reached toward the door to feel if it was there. It was. Her fingers slid over its slick chalky surface. "I hate it." She could only whisper. "I can't stand it." She crumpled the paper in her fist.

The pinup, unwrinkled, was something different this time, a black girl, naked, lying on fur, her bottom raised provocatively in the air. Before she even had breakfast, Yvonne smoothed it out neatly and carried it down the stairway to the Housemother's room, holding it delicately between two fingers. Some girls saw her in the downstairs hallway. "What the hell's that?" one of them asked, a New York girl.

Yvonne showed her.

"I'm being persecuted. Someone's leaving pictures outside my door."

34

"She's cute," the girl said. "You should be flattered."

"I should be flattered by the attention, Miss Brandon," Yvonne said to the Housemother, "but I'm not."

Miss Brandon was heavyset. She had been on the campus since 1948. She traveled mysteriously into Boston every Tuesday after lunch. As soon as she saw the picture, she laughed out loud.

But then when she asked Yvonne: "Have you got any idea who's doing it?" she sounded as if it could be Yvonne herself.

"How would I know? It isn't me."

"We never had a beauty queen on the campus before," the Housemother said indignantly.

"It's terrible. The girl doing it has lots of problems. Actually I feel very sorry for her." Humility! But the words stretched out in front of her like a beautiful finger, pointing at Miss Brandon herself. Speak no evil. See no evil. Yvonne, a future witch.

"I'll clear it up."

Said almost too confidently.

But if she couldn't stop it?

And if she could?

Which was more frightening?

It stopped.

But then in the dining room there were sudden silences.

At that table? No, at an unoccupied table where there had been silence before Yvonne walked into the room and there would be silence again after she left. The tables and chairs themselves sat there silent, beautiful too, with small delicate legs, adequate curves. Every chair in the dining room, every table, every bowl and cup was identical. Every chair designed for sitting, every bowl

35

designed for holding food. Every girl in the room sat properly on her chair, legs together.

Julie and Marilyn Henton came over and sat down, Marilyn with chocolate pudding and whipped-cream topping on her tray.

Yvonne had fruit cup.

"I wish I could diet." Marilyn was busty, dark-haired, a graduate of the Bronx High School of Science. "I wish God had given me my drives in the right direction. Maybe I need different drives. I don't want to give up some of the ones I have."

"Wait till you're married." Julie had chocolate pudding too. "You'll give them up."

"Miss Rhode Island here." Marilyn was one girl who dared say the words "Miss Rhode Island" out loud. "Food isn't a problem for her."

"I've got other problems."

"What, trying to come on like a virgin for Miss America?"

"They don't care if you're a virgin, for God's sake. I've got ice skating to worry about, Catullus. I have to translate twenty more poems before the final." At the identical tables, was only Yvonne different? "Do you think I look like a virgin?"

"That's why they chose you. You were the only girl there who could pass for one."

Letter from Mrs. Melli of the Rhode Island committee: "I know how hard it is to maintain the bearing expected of Miss Rhode Island and keep up with your studies at the same time, especially with all the temptations at Wellesley, all that marijuana, and still get ready for the pageant and practice your talent over and over again. That's a problem our girls have every year."

"Cut insulting me, Marilyn." Yvonne reached across

36

the table and snapped her finger in front of Marilyn's nose. "Since I became Miss Rhode Island everybody feels free to come down on me."

"Watch it, Marilyn." Julie was planning to study law. "She could sue you for defamation of character."

Your character shows only after you've been chosen. Quote from Mrs. Melli.

"Anyway, what does it matter if they think you're a virgin," Julie said, "you'll make your money out of it anyway."

"Do you make money?" Marilyn stopped eating. "I can ask, I'm a friend."

"She makes a lot, fifty dollars an appearance. She makes money every time she shows up somewhere."

"Do you really, Yvonne?"

Two girls at the next table looked as though they were listening to the conversation.

"Of course I do, that's the value of it." She should shout it all over the dining room. "I make more than fifty. A hundred, sometimes two hundred. If I get to be Miss America it's two hundred fifty minimum probably, maybe even five hundred."

"How much have you made so far?"

"Three fifty from personal appearances. But I've got something Easter that'll bring in two hundred more. I'm just stashing it away in the bank. You didn't know I was rich. Next summer I could make two thousand, three thousand, it depends on what I do. Plus I got twenty-five hundred dollars in scholarship money. That helps. My brother started Brown this year." At the next table the two girls were definitely listening. They were not even pretending to talk to each other. That didn't make Yvonne lower her voice, though. "If I work at Jordan Marsh, I make two hundred a week, cosmetics. Ten

37

weeks, two thousand dollars. Or I could do Historic Newport or Historic Wickford. I think I'll do Historic Newport, that's the best bet. It doesn't pay much, but they judge on that sort of thing. And if I win the pageant, it means a ten-thousand-dollar scholarship and sixty thousand more out of personal appearances."

"I think I'll come see it. When is it, September?" Often it was difficult to tell when Marilyn was being sarcastic.

"No, don't do that, too many people are coming already."

If anyone from Wellesley came, she would fall during the talent show. She would slap the face of the master of ceremonies when he asked, "Do you have a regular boyfriend?"

Why is that so?

The average Wellesley girl had participated in 2.4 community activities during high school. Yvonne had participated in 4: the Gilbert Stuart Memorial Birthplace, Muscular Dystrophy, Drill Team, and Stop the War. The average Wellesley girl had a 2.9 academic average. Yvonne's was 3.4 and that included a 3.6 in Classical Greek.

The average Wellesley girl didn't have a firm idea of her career direction. Yvonne knew her career choice.

The average Wellesley girl received one, maybe two phone calls from a boy each week and went out with a boy seven-tenths of a time per week, the sociology department had conducted a poll. Yvonne received six, maybe seven to ten calls, some she didn't even answer.

"I'd prefer it if nobody from Wellesley came." Yvonne spoke very distinctly.

Why?

Doesn't Harvard go down to New Haven when the football team plays there? If she were playing Bobby

38

Fischer for the chess championship, half of Wellesley would follow her to Iceland to see the game, they would watch her shuffle her pawns on TV, they would cheer every time her queen knocked off a knight.

"Listen," Marilyn said, "I'm not kidding. I could get a couple of carloads of girls from Wellesley and come down. You need a cheering section. All those Southern- ers, they have half of Mississippi coming up to cheer them on, the white half. What have you got?" She scraped back her chair. It made a raw noise. "Don't you think Wellesley could use something like this? It would bring the boys around. It's good for the image, I'm tired of being only smart."

"Oh, you wouldn't get anyone from Wellesley to go along. They don't care about Miss America." Sometimes Julie spoke with a drawl, it was almost Southern. She was from Hartford. Where did she get it? "They think it's anti-feminist. It's got no social content."

"You would put in social content." Marilyn had just taken a spoonful of chocolate pudding, but she didn't wait to answer. "Give your scholarship money to Black Studies. You could pledge it before you win."

"I need the money myself." Yvonne stood up even though her lunch was only half eaten. She put her crum- pled napkin on her tray. As she was leaving them every- body could see clearly: She was the most beautiful girl in the room. "I don't want anyone from Wellesley to come down. I'd hate it, I'll have plenty of people coming down to cheer from Rhode Island. I have to deal with them." She walked away from the table, out of the dining hall. She walked past the parlor, past the Housemother's office back up the staircase to her room.

There would be a busload of people coming down from Providence to Atlantic City and another bus chartered by L'Union St. Jean Baptiste of Woonsocket. The North Kingstown High School band was going to march down the boardwalk playing the Rhode Island Fight Song. They had it all planned, the committee, Mrs. Melli, Representative Ashkenazy, they were meeting, they were deciding, plotting on everything, It was time for a black winner, were they sorry they hadn't chosen Nelda Mack of Providence as Miss Rhode Island? Black is beautiful? She could hear them all over Rhode Island: A nigger, they chose a nigger this year, imagine that, it had to come. I don't think she's much, she's all right if you like colored, but I wouldn't touch one.

What did it matter to her, she was their nigger, everybody's nigger, and when she wasn't being their nigger, they were being hers. "Oh, Miss Rhode Island, you beautiful, with you blond curly hair, let me touch it, ain't she an angel, ain't she a doll."

But she was going to win.

She could feel it in her room as she walked into it. She could see it in the mirror. Looking directly at her, the smiling face proclaiming: She is going to win. Julie was still downstairs talking about her. That meant ten minutes of privacy. In ten minutes she could practice the walk down the runway.

Face front. A frontal. Then a pivot.

Then the rear view, up to the count of four. Should she wear the same sea-blue bathing suit? Her backside in it perfectly shaped, like an upside-down heart.

To keep the face from showing nervousness, recite a poem. Maybe something out of high school. But the lips couldn't move. Moving lips were the sign of a loser.

During the walk, the proper rhythm: Give me your tired, give me also your poor. Your huddled masses yearning to be free. Keep the arms from swinging, remember the smile. I lift my lamp beside the golden door. That takes her up to the end of the runway. Repeating it slowly takes her all the way back to face the judges again.

Always smiling.

Because she is going to win.

Walking down the runway, I can see it. Receiving the big bouquet of American Beauty roses.

Cutting the ribbon. I can feel it. On the cheeks, a heavy kiss from the mayor of every town. A hug from the governor; his embrace is thorough.

I can hear it, the whispering, each night before falling asleep: This is it, you won it, sixty thousand dollars.

This is it, your year's tour, all across America.

This is it, Victoria Pulchritudo, this is it, the most wonderful year of your life.

III

Who is she and where is she, the fierce maiden who stalks among the dune grasses, the weedy one who summons the fish in their hundreds in from the sea to climb onto the shore gasping for air, who brings the men and women down from the cities onto the beach calling them out one by one past the undertow into the deep water, summoning them to float among the sharp rocks, across the swiftly flowing breachways? She is the one who invites the boatmen past the hidden reefs, past the breakwaters into the harbor of refuge; but there a surprise is waiting.

Is she here?

Once, Yvonne remembered, a man driving a Mustang had to swerve, he was looking at her. On Route 1 north of Wickford. Behind him a trailer truck with its ferocious grinding, the sullen noise of braking, loud curses. Yvonne had looked both ways before crossing. She at least had proceeded with caution.

Was it you? Or was it your friend, is he still alive?

I was out of town at the time, it couldn't have been me. Go slow.

Just like Fino in his personal approach.

But now something was making him change, he was speeding up. On the way to the ice-skating rink he drove his MG like a wild man.

"You drive me crazy," he said to Yvonne when they got inside. "I never went out with anybody as pretty as you." He lit one of his cigarettes. They looked like very thin cigars. As if to protect her complexion, he carefully blew his smoke away from her face.

"Come on, I'm not that pretty, you'd think I was Helen of Troy." She was not in a graceful position, leaning too far forward, straining as she bent over to hook up the laces of her skates.

Fino's response: a wolf whistle. Embarrassingly loud.

But let the judges judge.

It's a good thing that they weren't judging now. Yvonne was grunting while she wrenched the laces tight, hooking them up back and forth. The beauty queen hot and red-faced. But soon her blades would be cutting into the cool and beautiful ice.

Fino was speedy, but she beat him out onto the rink.

Because there was no ashtray he had to stub out his cigarette on the wooden bench.

Smooth o'er the ice. Gliding along. The two of them together.

The ice was the color of the stones at Moonstone Beach, a variable white, translucent. Her arms, beneath a sweater, were stone-colored too, rosy quartz. "Could you go just a little bit slower?" Yvonne said. Fino wobbled.

The music brushed against her like wind. Fino skated her around a curve. Put your right foot in, put your right foot out. She could do it, even skating backward. Would he trip?

43

He couldn't waltz on ice, he couldn't dance. But he could attempt to skate forward, holding her while she skated backward.

"I'd like to skate alone now," she said.

Left leg out in front a little, not too far. Then a spin on the right. The left for balance, up and back, lowering with every turn. Slightly suggestive, with Fino watching, perfectly still.

Sudden applause: "That was terrific."

Yvonne answered him with her smile, the one she was planning to use on the judges. Beautiful but not very big.

The next trick was harder. One: work up speed. Two: slowly raise one foot behind to gain balance, leaning forward. Three: maintain position to the count of ten. Four: work up speed again. Five: repeat but leave the foot up to the count of fifteen. A slow fifteen. Now, same trick but skate an S. Not so easy.

Oh, Fino, did you ever think you'd get even the time of day off a girl like this?

Arms up, he began skating toward her as if to embrace her.

Until she shook her head. No. She was sweating, an athlete in training. Little bells like a child's, tied onto her skates, would remind her of her obligations. Cigarettes, no. Grass, not anymore. Drinking, no danger. Late hours, occasionally. The opposite sex, in moderation. No playing around for Miss Rhode Island. She skated away from him.

In the corner, a little girl, eight or nine, in a beige skating suit, began to practice the spin Yvonne had just completed. Blond hair too, long legs, but no more than just pleasant-looking.

Fino skated up toward Yvonne, trying again. He was playing a game, she was working. He reached out for her

44

hand. She skated away anyway, pushing forward, her arms spread out beside her like Winged Victory.

Left leg. Right leg. Up the runway.

But he was coming after her again.

It wasn't the smartest thing to do, making everyone else scat out of his way, as if he were driving his MG. Around another curve, hockey skating, swift as the wind. He was going to head her off at the pass.

That was his sense of humor.

Foolish games.

Ha, ha, but none of it's funny.

Who tripped first, Yvonne or Fino?

What does it matter, she was the one who screamed.

He only grunted.

Their legs were tangled. She could feel his skate grind into her leg, her leg was bleeding, it would leave a scar.

He began to roll away from her, but while he was doing it his skate pushed against her. It ripped her stocking.

"Are you O.K.?" He was up on his knees, the blades of his skates pointing upward. Some other skaters stood over her, whispering. Miss Rhode Island, are you going to die? Now in the spring before your time is up?

No answer.

Why the silence? She didn't bump her head, she didn't have a concussion. She couldn't have, she landed on her arm.

Somebody bent down beside her and started to help her up.

Another scream from Miss Rhode Island. Didn't you hear it? Echoing off the cliff at Matunuck, climbing the wooden walls of the mills at Pascoag? Her head moved and her legs, her neck moved. A man hitched his hands around her back, he brushed against her breast. Her shoulders moved, they swerved from side to side.

45

But one arm refused to follow.

Maybe it was broken.

Her face was as pale as the ice.

This sound, not a scream, halfway between that and a groan: "I can't move it."

That's why they had to carry her. Skating over the ice. Lucky people, touching Miss Rhode Island. Poor injured twig, bruised, a bruised flower, bear it tenderly.

Fino held on to her skates.

The sling: an oversize silk scarf from France, it cost $27.50. Bonwit Teller. A rust-colored border; inside it swirling blue flowers. A gift from Fino. The price tag was still on it.

The cast: pure white, nobody was allowed to autograph it. Autographs were out. Yvonne's own autographing hand was out of commission. Her lipstick-brushing hand. Her combing hand. The hand that had stroked Poulos just where he wanted it, more than once.

The arm, broken. A fracture of the radial head. The forearm, particularly, the posterior forearm, an almost purple color. The rest, unnaturally white under the white cast, the perfect body imperfect now, as flawed as anyone else's.

"But I don't give a shit about that aspect of it. I can't move it, that's what's getting to me."

"I'd like to draw a shamrock on the cast for you, something pretty." Julie was Irish. That's why she always seemed to be cheerful. "It'll pep you up." Even though the rule was no decorations on the cast. Nothing. "You have to mind it, I'm sure you do. You were perfect before, now you're not."

"I was never perfect."

Miss Rhode Island admitted it. And when Julie could

46

not see her, that night in the dark in bed she untied the silk scarf she was using for a sling and spread it out all the way so that it completely covered her face.

Her arm might not heal.

Proof: Under the cast the skin kept getting whiter. Whenever the doctor took off the cast, Yvonne thought of Nelda Mack, Miss Black Is Beautiful. It made her ashamed.

"In six months you won't even remember you broke it," the doctor said.

But doctors can be wrong. Everybody knows that.

"Does it hurt all the time?" Every day at the dinner table Julie cut up Yvonne's meat into little pieces.

"No, but I'm always thinking: It's broken."

The hills erode, the beaches wash out. The houses decay. Memory dwindles. Bodily strength is lacking. Pleasure is destroyed. Cicero said it, *De Senectute.*

"Don't you have to get up to go to a nine o'clock class?"

"Leave me alone, I'm cutting today."

"You ought to go to the infirmary. I'm going to get a doctor up here."

"My head aches, that's all." Her head, the winning head.

"Two days in a row? You've got a virus."

"I don't have a temperature."

"Listen, Yvonne, if you don't do something about this, then I'm going to."

Most popular, most beautiful. Had she been chosen for this?

"It's not that I don't understand what you're feeling. I broke my toe when I was eight and I still don't like to walk on the beach barefoot. I get nervous about stones. Once it happens you don't forget it."

47

Does the soldier ever forget the wound? There is mastectomy and there is radical mastectomy. Neither one can be forgotten. The spot where the mole will grow on the chin. There is less perfect. Then there is even less perfect.

"At least you should talk to your friend Fino sometime when he calls."

"I don't want to see him."

"He feels bad."

"I feel bad too."

Most-popular girls are never unavailable to their friends, or to their former friends. They never sit alone at dinner with an angry look on their faces warning everyone to stay away. They never go down to dinner at 6:55, just before the dining-room door closes, so that they don't have to sit with anyone else.

Most-likely-to-succeed girls do not cut classes and stay in their rooms, even on days when it is gray outside and stormy, when the tide on distant Moonstone Beach surges wildly and crashes onto the sand, and in Wellesley the trees wave back and forth in the wind and the girls, their classmates, move back and forth also, hour after hour, across the quadrangles, their long hair blowing in the wind.

Most-beautiful girls move slowly, but they move nevertheless. Their hips swivel gently, their lashes rise up and down, their smile appears and then it is gone.

Like Venus Genitrix, who is always moving over the earth and over the people on it.

But Yvonne is lying on her bed with her broken arm carefully resting at her side, no weight on it.

"Are you still here?"

"No, I'm somewhere else."

48

"Come off it, Yvonne, are you sick? Are you getting your period?"

"I'm just tired."

"Shall I bring you some coffee or something?"

"I'm studying, don't think I'm not studying."

Though it took all afternoon to translate one line of Catullus. "He is changed to a god, he who looks on her." That's what it said in the trot. But what exactly did it mean?

The morning she came down to breakfast without brushing her hair, Marilyn asked her, "Have you gone hippie?"

"I can't, it hurts my arm, it's difficult for me."

Now there was whispering not silence when she walked into the dining room. Progress! "What a bitch of an accident," a girl she didn't know said to her in the food line. They could approach her. Miss Rhode Island wounded. She had been brought down to their level. The head of the Feminist Union even came up to console her. "Listen, I don't think much of beauty contests, you better believe it." She was an attractive, overcompetent girl who always wore three rings on one hand. "But I'm sorry it happened, I bet it hurts like hell."

"Not so much anymore. Except for the first week. It hurt a lot then."

If the Venus de Milo still had her arms, they would be angry at her too.

That's what they start with, the arms.

Then what? The breasts.

Or old age takes care of it for them.

"Alas, how the swift years glide away!" Horace, Book II, Ode 14. Sight translation. Her grade: 65 out of a possible 100.

"It's not a beauty contest, it takes work." The head of the Classics Department was a man in his sixties, getting too old.

"I got a little mixed up on the gerund."

"And the accusative here too, you messed that up."

Perhaps she could make a living as a model for *Vogue*. Her eccentricity: one arm was always hidden.

But how did Kirby ever find out?

No matter. He invited her to go ice skating with him so he could show it to the people on TV. Beauty queen with a broken arm. She's had some tough luck, but she keeps on going.

"I still want to do the best I can so I don't let Rhode Island down," Yvonne said over the air. As they were skating around the rink, Kirby kept his arm around her. He patted her hip. "Thanks for calling," she said to him after the show was over. But he didn't call back.

As a result, her arm started aching again, a nerve ache, and one evening when Julie was out of the room, the pain made her cry. Real tears came.

"It was very nice of you to think of me," she said when a photographer from the Boston *Globe* telephoned to ask her to pose for a picture at the skating rink with her arm in the flowered sling. Plucky Wellesley girl, Miss Rhode Island keeps on skating for Miss America Pageant. "I can't let Rhode Island down," queen with broken arm says. But this time it wasn't so difficult to balance on skates with one arm in a sling.

The next week the photographer called her again. "Thirty-four papers across the country have picked up the picture and carried it." Did any other Miss Rhode Island ever get so much out-of-state publicity before?

Thirty-four newspapers.

Everybody saw it.

50

Julie's mother sent it to her from Hartford, and Julie posted the clipping on the Pomeroy bulletin board.

"I don't want any pinups," Yvonne said angrily after she ripped it down. "I have to look at the damn cast, I don't want to look at a picture of it too."

At Walpole, at the Correctional Institute, four young men prisoners, presently incarcerated, saw it too. Marilyn was with her when she picked up her mail and read their letter. It was typed on paper lined like a prison uniform.

> The walls close in
> The night is dark
> Yet Yvonne will always light a spark.
> Your perseverance
> Your beauty too
> Comforts us the whole night through.
> Your picture is our treasure
> We kiss it each night
> We fondle it gently
> We treat it right.

"I love it." Marilyn took the poem out of her hand. "When you have your fiftieth birthday, you can take it out and read it again, every night."

Yvonne grabbed it back. "I hate it, I'm going to tear it up, I'm going to throw it away." But before doing that, she put it for a while into a manila folder that was marked Miss Rhode Island Souvenirs.

In Providence, Truston Clapp saw the picture. In Boston, Poulos. In Wickford, her father saw it; he called her from the office, he gave her a kiss over the phone. A big kiss, the kind he used to give.

"I don't know why I did it. I shouldn't have let him take

51

my picture, I don't even look good in it, they don't leave me alone, this thing is horrible, I'm sorry I got into it, I hate it, I'll be glad when it's over. I go out with a boy, he breaks my arm for me. I don't want to go out anywhere. I don't like being Miss Rhode Island. I don't want to be Miss America. I don't want to be on display in front of everybody, I don't think I want that. Do I want that? Is that what I want?"

"It's all right, you're doing fine." A father's comfort. "You're handling it O.K. Not every girl could deal with it. You're doing terrific. I'm proud of you."

And then, over the phone, the thrilling, powerful sound: another kiss.

Electric. Almost as good as the real thing.

Those kisses, do you remember them? That's what a girl needs when she's feeling low, father love, what's better for a girl than that? What's better than a father who appreciates you, he calls you princess, he wants to dance with you, he never opens his mouth to shush you, you're five years old and furious, you shout it out, crying, a grown-up shout: "No, I'm not, I'm not a girl!" A father, be thankful if you had a father who loved you and cared for you. Did you have one or didn't you? Maybe a grandpa? Maybe a kitty, a doggy? That's how it starts out, with your father, a father, and now she was Miss Rhode Island. Even with a broken arm, Miss Rhode Island. Even with all her doubts. Every girl in Rhode Island was beautiful, but she was the most beautiful of all. In Rhode Island: water, earth, stones, grass, breasts, hair, teeth, legs, trees. Portuguese, Italians, Yankees, Jews. And out of this she was chosen, Providence chose her. Pulchritudo, she was Pulchritudo's darling. She still was, twenty years after she pushed her way, red and slime-covered, bubbling and groaning, through the matted hairs, onto the waiting hands of the man, the obstetrician, who slapped her and held her upside down, scrawny and blotched, so lean from her exertion that her vulva protruded, shockingly, an announcement when they looked at her to see if she was a girl or a boy. The first child: a girl. Miss Rhode Island.

IV

Queen of the Quisset Club! It looked like a castle. On a point of land sticking into the bay. The pale blue gown —she had to be her cousin's bridesmaid in June—a little unsophisticated. But one arm in a sling, that was enough to make it look all right.

It was possible to open the heavy front door of the club with the left hand. Inside on the stairway landing there was a big window facing over the water. Like in Yvonne's own house. Her mother had finally promised: someday Yvonne could have her own wedding at home instead of in church so she could gaze at the ocean as she walked down to get married.

The contact: Mr. Clapp. He was standing at the bottom of the staircase, the president, easy to spot, the man in charge, the one holding a cigar. Heavyweight crew, squash, push-ups—he looked like the son of a member, the grandson.

"You must be Yvonne." His smile appeared total. "I'm Truston Clapp." And right away, wild, he leaned over and kissed her on the cheek. Not just a kiss of greeting either, but softer, a more private kiss.

A sophisticated girl might know exactly how to respond. Yvonne pointed to her sling. "I didn't bring

54

along the Miss Rhode Island crown. With this thing it seemed silly to wear it."

"Everybody will know who you are." He helped her off with her coat. "You're the most beautiful one here." Actually, it was her mother's coat, white rabbit, three-quarter length, perfect for over a gown. "You must get tired of hearing that kind of thing. But I have to say it."

"I'm getting used to it."

"Then you're not letting it scare you."

But it did.

"Is there somebody I should give the coat check to?" She could feel the weight when he put his arm around her and walked her toward the checkroom. He was just the slightest bit heavyset, and on the dark side.

"I'll take it. I came here by myself."

But when the checkroom girl handed him the ticket, he put it into his pants pocket. Right next to his thigh. And then he patted the spot where it was.

In the ballroom a band was playing. Red and white chrysanthemums formed an arch over the door. A red satin ribbon hung down from the staircase; Quisset Club, 1891, it said. No Doucette had ever got past the front door there before.

"I get the honor of the first dance. I'm your official host." The cigar went into an ashtray. "Unless you'd like to have a drink first."

"Miss Rhode Island can't drink in public."

"Maybe I'll slip her a little something when nobody's looking."

"Miss Rhode Island shouldn't even do it on the sly."

"O.K., then I'll take you dancing. You can do that, right?"

Yvonne wiggled her sling. "So long as this doesn't fly off. I hope it's fast, I love fast dancing."

"Then we'll make it fast." He was a fire-eater! "But I have to warn you, I once won a Charleston contest."

"You don't scare me."

With the flat of his hand on her back—it was almost bare, only netting covered it, only netting and a little lace —he steered her into the next room, toward the dancing. "You don't scare me either." He stopped walking and turned toward her for an instant. "And I thought you might."

"I thought I scared everybody." They were brushing past dancing couples. "Sometimes I think I scare my own mother, I know I scare my roommate." One dancer, a man in a plaid dinner jacket, broke away from his partner and bowed low to Yvonne. She had to slow down, she had to smile and bow back. "But nobody ever admits being scared, to me anyway."

"That shows you how scared they really are."

Now they were in front of the bandstand facing the band. Like a conductor's, his hand moved up and down in short choppy motions, commanding speed. To accommodate him the music shifted, swung, got faster.

Result: The Jersey Bounce. A disappointing selection.

"I haven't heard that since I was a kid."

"Is it an old song?"

"I'm not old!"

"I didn't say you were old." Shoulders back straight. Now the breasts showed well, even under the sling. "I didn't even imply it." It was mostly below the waist Yvonne moved. Her honorarium: $100. The Quisset Club was getting its money's worth. "I really appreciate your asking me."

"I decided to early on, but I was sure I was right the minute I saw your picture in the paper."

56

"Which picture? The ice-skating one! I hated it."

"Well, I loved it." With his hand on her waist, he twirled her away from him and then back. "You seemed as if you needed protection. It made me want to hold you."

To keep the rhythm of the dance, they were looking at each other.

"And now I am."

Of the two, it was Yvonne who looked away first.

But then, quickly, she glanced back at him again.

He was still looking directly at her. Already it was apparent.

The president of the Quisset Club was hoping to make her.

"Isn't there some kind of ceremony I'm supposed to be in?"

"A Grand March. I take you down the aisle and then I give you a bouquet. It's a tradition. Has been since 1895."

"Now I wish I'd brought my crown." Did that sound childish? "I like ceremonies, I like flowers. What kind of flowers?"

"Roses probably." From dancing so fast he was panting a little. "It'll get you ready to be Miss America."

"Nothing will ever get me ready for that."

"Oh yes." They were both jumping up and down. "I know what will."

"What's that?" The Jersey Bounce seemed to be reaching its climax.

"You need to enjoy yourself more."

No lie!

Was he planning to do it in Providence? In an apartment high up with a view of the State House out of the

57

bedroom window? At Little Compton maybe? At Moonstone or Weekapaug? "How can I enjoy myself? I can't until this shitty contest is over."

"Sure you can." The music was shifting. Now it was becoming an old-fashioned fox-trot. "Just get your mind off it."

Maybe at Newport overlooking the harbor. Maybe at Arcadia State Park, deep in under the trees. But not upstairs at Pomeroy Hall at Wellesley during unlimited visiting hours, with Julie impatiently studying in the library.

The dancing had slowed. They were rocking, hardly moving. "What house are you in at Wellesley?"

He had very dark eyes. Deep-set. They didn't look away, they looked at. To. They looked in.

"Pomeroy." She didn't look away either.

"I'd like to take you to dinner Tuesday."

"Monday's when my cast comes off." White armor over the pure flesh. "You can get to see the real me."

"What's the best time to pick you up?"

"Six." The answer was so direct she had to look down toward the floor. "Maybe six-thirty."

Had he come at last?

Him, the expected one. Mr. Rhode Island.

What a surprising choice!

And now, through everyone's mind the question is gliding, sharp and swift as the runners of a skate.

In this day and age could Miss Rhode Island still be a virgin?

But if she wasn't, could she become Miss America?

Did Truston imagine it, like her father and mother?

Or did he already know the answer?

"Let's go."

He picked her up in front of the drugstore on Washington Street, Wellesley, Not at Pomeroy Hall. With the car motor running, a low beating sound. "First we'll go have some dinner. I'll find a nice restaurant."

"I could go to McDonald's, I don't care." The safety belt tight around her, the buckle shining and heavy on her soft lap. No more accidents for Miss Precious. En garde!

"Do you really want to go to McDonald's? At least it's fast."

"Why not! That's where Miss America's supposed to eat." And there among the yellow tables there would be children, they would not stare at her.

But while she was sitting at a table waiting for him to come back from the food line, a little black girl—six years old maybe, oversized, puffy, with meager pigtails—leaned over to her from the next table and said, "You very pretty."

"Thank you." Cruelly Yvonne looked away. But only for a minute. She forced herself to turn back. "You're pretty too." But it had taken too long.

"You're the best-looking one here." Truston leaned over and kissed her on the forehead. He couldn't touch her. The tray was in his hands.

"I was wrong, people look at me here too, they keep staring, that kid over there keeps staring at me, it's like the dining hall at Wellesley, everybody staring at me, like animals, they can't keep their eyes off me, they don't let go."

"People like to look at you."

"They shouldn't, they should leave me alone, it's like I'm a movie they're watching, look at her." The black girl was staring. "She's got her mouth open."

59

"That's because she admires you." Truston put down Yvonne's hamburger and her coffee, neatly in front of her. He spread a paper napkin and emptied a bag of French fries onto it.

"I hate it when they look. It makes me lose my appetite. I want to kill them. They wouldn't like it if somebody kept staring at them all the time." She leaned forward over the table. Her face was flushed, her hair almost touched the coffee cup. "It makes my skin crawl."

"Don't let it bother you. Everybody's like that. I'm like that. If I see something beautiful, I want to stare. It's like the ocean. When it's in sight, you have to keep looking at it, right?"

"I'm not the ocean." Yvonne pulled her coffee cup closer. But she didn't drink. Coffee caused bad breath. Even in beauty queens.

"You're better than the ocean. And I love the ocean. I've got a cottage on the beach. I even go down there in the winter. Sometimes I even go into the water in the wintertime. I can't keep away from it." He put his hand over hers. His hand was warm. "Matunuck. Do you know where that is?"

"Down near Moonstone Beach."

"The house is right on Moonstone."

Natural beauty—for that Yvonne could smile. "I've walked by those houses."

"I'd like to take you down there."

The blood of the Arnolds, modesty. She looked down at the table. "O.K." Vee, vee—in her mind she could still hear the car motor going.

"Right after we eat," Truston said. He squeezed her hand.

The black girl and her mother were leaving. The

mother was pushing a coat onto the girl. The girl was twisting around to stare at Yvonne.

"I'm tired of being Miss Rhode Island."

"I think you really love it."

"But it's like there's a war going on all the time. Them against you. The beautiful ones on one side; the rest of the world on the other side. Do you think I'm paranoid?"

His hand moved up, slowly, to her arm. "No, I don't think so."

"I can't be myself, everyone grabs me. As if they want to take me over."

But he didn't take his hand away. She could feel it on her arm, waiting. She could feel it in these places too: between her legs, beneath her stomach, at the side of her breasts. His thumb was stroking, back and forth.

"I don't mean you. But everybody expects something out of me."

"You don't have to give it."

"They expect me to be mean to them." Her voice began to shake. "The girls especially. It's like they all own me. Even the girls."

"They're wrong." His hand moved up and down along her forearm, over the bones that had been broken. Slow, steady, it was like a cure. With his other hand he began stroking her knees under the table. "Nobody owns you," he said.

"I feel like crying."

"Come out into the car."

His arm around her, she walked out to the parking lot. Her eyes were almost shut. But no crying came until the car moved out onto the highway, headed south toward Rhode Island.

Fortunately, there was a box of Kleenex on the seat beside her.

There wasn't much traffic heading down.

In Dedham she started sobbing. But it also sounded like coughing. She covered her face with her hands. When he said, "Don't be embarrassed," she started crying loud, the tears ran down her cheeks, she wiped them away with Kleenex, she wiped her mouth, her lipstick came off, all of it. She twisted around in her seat, facing first toward the ocean and then westward, toward the place where America was.

In Norwood she leaned her head back against the seat and moaned.

In Walpole she whispered: God.

In Foxboro the sounds that came out were like gasps. "I'm getting your car messy." There were damp wads of Kleenex all over the floor.

"That's all right."

We know: Crying like that, it is like an orgasm, the first one after a long time. It's like coming again and again, finally, after a difficult month.

In North Attleboro, there were little sobs, diminished, little sobs interrupted with giggles from time to time. "I don't know what's the matter with me. I don't act like this."

"You were never Miss Rhode Island before."

By the time they passed through the town where her father worked, where the Swank plant stood, its dark windows like blank eyes against the cold night, the crying had almost stopped.

She was breathing deeply.

By the time they crossed the border speeding on the highway into Rhode Island, cutting over the Massachusetts line in the dark night among the anonymous trees, all the crying was done.

To get to the cottage, this is how you go. Take Route

1 south past Wickford in the darkness. The weeping has ended, they cannot hear it, it was in another state. Go over Tower Hill past the road to the peninsula where the Quisset Club stands. Along the highway that marks the line where the glacier stopped. Down to the beachfront land, deep-loamed, built up beyond the glacial lands, down the beach road south over the new-made land almost to the edge of the sea, down the road west along the sea, down past the pond, down to the dunes where the cottage stands, one of a row of big brown shingled cottages, the ones that survived after the great hurricane. These won, those lost. And out of the damp, half-heated, shadowy cottage, carrying a blanket and an enormous soft sleeping bag, down onto the dunes of Moonstone Beach.

Tuesday evenings.

The second Tuesday. "I rented a motel room here on Route 9."

The third Tuesday. The same motel, a different room. It overlooked a row of ranch houses, the houses where husbands had watched patiently Yvonne's image smiling on the TV.

"I've got exams, I'm falling behind. I don't think I can win. They get all these girls from Texas, Mississippi."

Truston took the pillow off the bed and hit her with it. But very gently. "You'll win. Rhode Island money is as good as Texas money any time."

"There's not so much of me, I'm not so big."

An invitation. Inspection, first on the right, second on the left. Then carefully both together. "You're crazy." He ran the flat of his hand over her mouth. "Don't say things like that." That was one hand. The other had moved elsewhere.

63

It made her bite his finger, buck her legs up.

He didn't have a young body, but he wasn't flabby. "I'll just tell you what to do and you do it. And you'll win."

That was not something a college boy would ever say.

"Just think about this when you walk down the runway." He put her hands, both of them, there. "And when you do your ice skating, think about this." He rolled over on top of her and hitched her legs up.

"When I do my ice skating I have to think about the figures I'm doing."

He pushed into her.

"Not true."

She lay perfectly still.

"You think about this."

"All right."

"Ice-skate."

"What do you mean?" But she knew. Furthermore, she wasn't embarrassed about it either.

"Come on, go ahead, right now."

"Like this?"

"Move your arms too."

When she did, a great chill came over her.

As if she had already won.

Miss America!

The competition ended! Immortality achieved!

Doesn't Miss America get listed in *Who's Who?*

And doesn't she stay in after her year is ended?

Elizabeth Cady Stanton, Molly Pitcher. Julia Ward Howe, Clara Bow, Mother Seton. Above the halls at Wellesley they sit in the heavens looking down at the girls. They will never be forgotten, they will never disappear into the earth along with their classmates, along with all the other Doucettes, those of the past and the present.

"One kiss will make us both immortal. That's how it works. Modern people don't pay any attention to immortality, but the Romans cared, that's why they've lived so long, monuments more enduring than bronze, that's why I like studying Latin."

First he will look, then he will touch, then he will move close to her, leg to leg. The air disappears, the light is gone, nothing sounds but his breath, there is no color but his skin's, his icy eyes', then he will press forward to her; history is wiped out, there is no Brown, no Harvard, there is no winning the race or losing, neither French nor English, neither beautiful nor ugly, neither then nor now.

Miss America in love.

"When I was looking out the window, I thought I saw you coming toward me, right across the quadrangle. It was night, it was crazy, you wouldn't be there. I must have been looking at somebody else."

"What day was it?"

"Friday evening. Right after dark."

"That's when I was thinking about you. Maybe thoughts travel."

"It must have been one of the campus cops. Maybe it was somebody on the faculty."

"I was walking home from the office. Up the hill. I kept thinking about your body. I kept thinking how beautiful you are."

B: Beauty.

L: Love.

Miss Rhode Island. April 17, Pomeroy Hall.

Self-improvement, A to Z.

A: Arms.

It had begun happening to her mother already, the looseness, in the upper arms, the hanging flesh. The way to deal with that was rotation, arms outspread, move them around and around, held stiffly, fifty times.

B: Bust. Hands at the waist, elbows moved back and forth, a smooth motion. This exercise may not be effective. However, they say it works better if you do one arm at a time. Twenty-five times, each side.

C: Chin. Perfect, a girl with a perfect chin. "I may not be so beautiful, but at least I have a perfect chin. My mother told me." The only thing to do with that was wash it properly, soap and water. Never mind creams, those are for old ladies.

D: Dimple. Lacking. Nor is there a way to provide one. D: Dress. The committee, Mrs. Melli, they had the budget for that. They were working on it.

But P: Personality.

"Don't you worry you'll get warped doing all those exercises?" Julie asked the day Yvonne reached L: Legs. A flutter exercise, stretched out on the floor on her stomach, legs up, kicking first one leg outward and then the other.

"I'm an athlete, I'm training." The kicking stopped. "If I were on a sports team it wouldn't seem funny. Think of me as a jock. In for the Olympics. You should do some with me, it'll take your mind off studying." Julie had confessed she was having difficulty studying. "This year I don't know why, I'm not succeeding at anything."

Julie's exercise now was polishing fingernails. She was doing it at Yvonne's desk, where the light was better. "I hate that sort of stuff. I'm never going to get fat anyway."

"You'll look better, you'll feel better." But there was a faint sweaty odor, now permanent, in all the leotards

Yvonne wore for her exercises. "Everybody should do exercises, Truston does exercises, I'm going to continue even if I don't win Miss America."

"You never did exercises last year."

"I didn't want to in front of you, you made me nervous, you still make me nervous about it."

"If you're going to win your contest . . ." Julie was working on the final thumb; she had to finish before she answered. But she finally looked up. "Then you have to be cool. You shouldn't let that bother you." She waved her hands to dry her nails; they were blood-colored. "Miss America wouldn't let it bother her."

Was she right?

Who cares? They don't judge on personality. L: Legs, that was more important. They judge on something else.

"I think your friend Truston's going to help you win." Every evening at dinner Marilyn talked about men.

"Do you think so?"

"I mean it. You seem happy for the first time since you broke your arm. Everyone says a woman in love is prettier. You know what that means."

A brief smile from Yvonne.

"Also a pregnant woman. Maybe you'll get knocked up in time for the contest."

"God, if I got an abortion, there'd be publicity."

"My father's a gynecologist. He'll take care of you. He'd love to. You can come to New York and get it there without any trouble. He once told me, 'I'll get you a D and C if you ever need it. You won't even have to tell your mother.' "

"I wouldn't go to anybody's father, that would be embarrassing."

"Why? They're all the same. They all love the same thing. They're all creeps. Miss America's gynecologist, he'd love that. Your boyfriend, that's what he likes too."

"He's not like that."

"Of course he's like that. Admit it, he likes you more because you're Miss Rhode Island."

"He's more sophisticated than that. You know what he once said to me? He said, 'I'd like you better if you worked in a mill.'"

"Did he say he'd like you better if you weren't Miss Rhode Island?"

"He said he'd like me better if I had a husband. How could I be Miss Rhode Island if I had a husband?"

"I see why you like him." Marilyn leaned all the way back in her chair. "He sounds sexy."

"He is sexy."

Mr. Busyfingers.

The fourth Tuesday evening.

Always pushing in one direction.

"You could get an apartment in Pawtucket in a three-family house. You could get a husband. You could get a job in a jewelry factory. I'd like it better that way." In his attaché case, he had brought a bottle of wine, and bread and cheese. He had a copy of the Providence *Journal* too. While they ate in the motel room they looked at the help-wanted ads. Carder, linker, racker, stringer. Gluer, polisher, plater, hand linker. "You could send your kids to the day care. Your husband would be out. Then you'd come home from work one day, you could say you're sick, and then I come up to your house. How about it?"

"No way. My father got out of that, he grew up in a three-decker house." Yvonne was naked. She set down her wineglass and put a blanket around her shoulders. "Woonsocket. No, thanks."

"Woon-sockette, a little Frenchie, that's what I always wanted."

68

"Watch out, Truston, I'll hit you with the bottle." But the bottle was out of reach. A pretend lunge for it.

What else could he do but grab both her wrists and push her down onto the bed, while she screamed, quietly, so people in the adjoining rooms couldn't hear. Would he break her arm too? The same arm? The other arm?

"Come off it, Truston, my mother was an Arnold, you ever hear the name Arnold in Rhode Island? That was my mother's name."

He let go. He sat up in the bed. "We must be related. I've got Arnolds back there."

"Out of William Arnold, he came before Roger Williams."

"Right."

"My God, it's incest, I'm half Arnold."

"I'm only a little bit. My father's grandfather." His hands into action again. "Admit it, you're just a Frenchie."

"It's incest! I've committed incest." Another weak scream. "It's as bad as being with my own father"—she pushed his hand away—"or my own brother. I'm the only Miss America who ever committed incest."

"The only one you know about."

"I'll be the only one related to Benedict Arnold too. Have you got him?"

"Yes, but his family went to Connecticut."

"So what, same family. I'll be the only Miss America who's Canadian too." She motioned to him to fill the wineglass. "I'll go to Canada first thing, I'll start in Quebec and I'll skate to Montreal, they skate on that river in the winter, I'll do a tour, Miss Quebec." When he handed her the wine, she took a good swallow. "I'll wear a big Q on my breast under my costume during the pageant. Right here." She pointed. "I'll put it on with lipstick, a Q on one breast and an RI on the other."

"And an F for Frenchie between your legs."

"Don't be dirty, you should be thankful you have Miss Rhode Island in bed with you, maybe Miss America, other men would commit murder to be in your place and you're insulting me, calling me a Frenchie."

"I'm complimenting you, not insulting you."

"Well, I'm not French, I'm American, Miss America, that's it."

"I'm going to make you that."

"Truston, I want to win." She took another drink of wine, this time only a sip, though.

"No, you don't, but I'm going to make you do it." He took the wineglass out of her hand.

"How can you do that?"

"Well, let's start out this way, you start out by kissing me right here."

"Right here?"

"I'm going to teach you how to win it."

Her mouth was busy, she couldn't talk. So she nodded her head.

"Truston wants me to win. That's why I put the map up there." Miss Loyalty, Yvonne would win that. A big map of the United States was taped up on the wall over her bed.

"I think it's ugly." Julie herself had an abstract above her bed. Paul Klee: a rudimentary face, muted colors, forms that seemed to fly away. "I bet you think I'm terrible to say that."

"No, not at all, just think of it as an abstract and then you'll like it." Massachusetts was purple, Rhode Island

70

green, the color of sixty, seventy thousand dollars. But Arizona was green too; so was Oregon. "Truston gave it to me, it's for good luck." If Rhode Island had been red, white, and blue, it would have been better. "It will help me win."

"I didn't know you were so competitive." Julie was a psych major. She was sitting at her desk with a book open in front of her, *Abnormal Behavior.* "Is that why you went into the contest? What was your real motive?"

"I already told you." Yvonne usually worked lying on her bed. At her right hand was a dictionary; at her left hand a notebook; beside her thigh a copy of Catullus. "I didn't have a choice, there wasn't any way for me to get out of it."

The book closed around Julie's finger. The pages above her hands were filled with paranoia, the pages below with depression. "It couldn't be that simple, you have to get something out of it."

"Well, I enjoy it."

"What do you enjoy most?"

"I don't have time for psychoanalysis, I have to finish this Latin."

"You want to avoid it."

"Damn it!" Up off the bed. "I enjoy Truston the most." Yvonne walked over to the desk where Julie was sitting and stood leaning over her, a superior body. Julie would never get fat, but she had too much belly, too much thigh spread on the chair. "You ought to throw that book out."

"You're just avoiding the answer. It must be difficult to deal with it."

"You're what's difficult to deal with."

Yvonne moved away, suddenly; swiftly she took off her

71

shirt. Now she was wearing only a bra and jeans. She walked over to the sink, she began washing her face. It made Julie reopen her book.

"Maybe it has something to do with competition."

"Don't jump to conclusions. I hate competition."

"Why are you in one?"

"You keep asking me." Yvonne's face was behind a towel. "If you want to find out, go into a contest yourself. You could be Miss Connecticut. Go ahead, you might like it." She put the towel down. "I've got a bruise on my knee, I bumped it." She took off her jeans, she began inspecting her knee, her panties were pale green with flowers on them, her bra was white, both were cut low; her little belly, curving, her breasts, almost bare, they began to get goose pimples on them, ice princess, why should she mind the cold! "What do you think this is?" Her leg up, her pink knees, she made Julie look.

"Just a black-and-blue mark. Don't be such a baby."

"It had better go away."

"Your arm healed all right, didn't it?"

"No, there's still a mark there, see." There for Julie to see if she looked carefully, she had to lean close, was a pale bluish tinge on the inside of the arm below the place where the bone had broken.

"Nobody's going to see that, for God's sakes. It'll disappear."

"You can't be sure."

"I thought you didn't care about the contest."

No answer. Yvonne put her hands behind her back, she unhooked her bra and threw it on the bed. Catullus: "And young girls no longer fearful come naked, walk before you singing praises, almighty god." Swift feet, white hands, was Julie even looking? A modest and beautiful girl under the rushing wings of the goddess, lifted up by feathers into that other place, no longer fearful.

"Aren't you getting chilly walking around like that?"

"I'm getting on my nightgown." Yvonne lifted up first one leg and then the other, removing the panties. Now she was naked.

Past the desk where Julie sat, past the bed where Julie lay each night, up to the window. Her soft and naked back toward Julie. She put her arms up, one on each side of the window frame. "There's a nice moon."

"The whole world can see you if you stand like that, Yvonne."

"Nobody's looking."

"I'll look up exhibitionism in the book."

"They can't see me." Yvonne spun around, her white arms whiter from the cold, her nipples stood out more, the skin of her thighs was tighter, the moon had shone on her breasts, now it shone on her shoulders, outdoors now, they couldn't see her, the only one who could see her was Julie. Truston had seen her that way, standing, her lips half open, Poulos had in a motel once, Fino had never seen her that way, certain, entire, like the Aphrodite of Cnidos, but with her hair let down, flowing around her shoulders. "Hand me my nightgown. It's on the closet door."

Julie was seated, Yvonne was standing. The closet was close to one, it was close also to the other. It was easy to reach, there was no reason to ask someone else to go to it. But Julie stood up to get the nightgown.

"You worried you'll get another bruise?"

Yvonne took it, she spread its skirt wide, it went over her head, hiding her white, deadly face, hiding her breasts, hiding the place where the Miss America contest

73

begins, the door, the seal, the evidence, was she a virgin? Did Miss America have it still? Was it there? The sacred hymen of which Catullus sang: Io hymen, hymenaea io, until the gown covered her down to the ankles. "I'm sleepy, I think I'll go to bed."

Julie shut her book. But before she could get undressed herself, she had to turn the desk lamp off.

Yvonne had a lamp on her bedside table.

Switch on for fingernail inspection. One cuticle is uneven. In the bedside drawer there is a file, she pushes the cuticle neatly in. Try to hide from her in darkness, you cannot.

Julie turns her naked back. Are her breasts sagging? You can imagine it, is her heart sagging too? In front of Miss Rhode Island, wouldn't your heart sag too, wouldn't it fall?

But these are the things that rise up before her:

The women, the old women calling her blessed.

The children and the little goddesses, their reflections above the clouds.

Pulchritudo, hovering over.

And I, I rise up at the thought of her. And you, no doubt you, rise up before her too.

V

"Fix me up with some Wellesley girls," Joseph said. "Fix me up with Miss Massachusetts."

For this she had come home over Easter vacation?

"Is that why you wanted to enter me?"

From Joseph a vulgar, coughing laugh.

"In the contest."

"God, it was just a joke."

"Some joke!" She looked away from him, out the living-room window, toward the bay. "You wouldn't like Miss Maine. New Hampshire goes steady. You might like Connecticut. But I didn't like her and I don't want to get in touch with her. I don't have time for it. I have too many things to do, I don't want to be bothered with that kind of stuff. I'm too busy."

There was a shopping center to be opened in Cranston. Miss Rhode Island cut the ribbon. There was a new branch of a home-improvement store to be opened in Middletown. There was an appearance at Jordan Marsh at Warwick Mall two shopping days before Easter, along with a model wearing an Easter Bunny suit.

"You're darling. You're sweet. I'm happy to shake your hand." The women shoppers came up, but the men shied away. Little boys dared, nine years old, ten years

75

old, up to twelve when they were white, even fourteen when they were Italian. But no real teen-agers. Except for a few who were black, gangs of three or four on their way to the record department. They came up to shake her hand, they giggled, they hit each other on the arms waiting in the line under the sign "Meet Miss Rhode Island." Afterwards, they could talk dirty about her.

One of the things that made Yvonne uneasy was this: Jordan Marsh was a branch of a Boston store. Even so, it was the biggest store in Rhode Island.

Another thing that made Yvonne uneasy was this: She represented the smallest state. Therefore she was chosen from among the smallest number of girls. Miss New York was one out of three-quarters of a million girls in the age bracket eighteen to twenty-three. She was one out of only forty thousand girls. Even fewer if you count only single girls. Even fewer if you count white girls only.

Not one of the forty thousand came up to shake her hand. Adolescents only, pre-teens, girls in high school. Only older women. Some were pregnant. When Yvonne suddenly, daringly patted one of these on the stomach, the woman blushed, she smiled, she was happy. Even a boy in there would benefit, and a girl would flourish, she would be beautiful. The touch straightened hooked noses, it rounded breasts, it kept the thighs firm, made the hair springier—just like in the commercials.

"They wanted their daughters to have a better bust line, they wanted me to rub their stomachs, but they didn't dare ask," she told her mother when she got home. She also told it to Truston when he picked her up at lunchtime for a quick sandwich in the cafeteria at the airport. "No one ever goes there," Truston promised her. "No one will see us. I'm as concerned to keep it quiet as you are. You're telling all those Wellesley girls.

76

I'm not telling anybody." And then after lunch he parked on a side road leading to the freight terminal, a strangely empty road, and kissed her and rubbed against her.

"I have to get back."

"Nobody's going to come."

"Nobody but you."

She pulled away.

Back to the women waiting in line to see her. They touched too, her arm, her shoulder. Some even hugged. "Isn't she something! Isn't she just a doll!" two women said, not to her but to each other. "Don't she look wonderful!"

"Good luck, I'm not going to stay. I won't hang around and bother you." Mrs. Melli, the official Miss Rhode Island chaperone, didn't wait in line. She went right up to Yvonne, unhooking the velvet rope that guarded her. And one old Portuguese woman—fat, a grandmother—took Yvonne in both arms, she pulled her toward her huge breasts, she kissed her on both cheeks. "Wonderful, wonderful, you'll win." She made the sign of the cross. And then at the end of the day another old woman came, like her but from some sort of Slavic race. She hugged too. Then with her finger she slowly traced the mark of a circle three times on Yvonne's forehead.

A girl with less poise would have been upset. A girl who wasn't in love. A girl who didn't have the support of a loyal family, the support of a brother like hers. Every day the first thing in the morning at breakfast the whole week of Easter vacation, as an apology for asking her to fix him up, he had said the same thing: "I know you're going to win it, Yvonne, I feel it in my bones"; until it became a joke by the end of the week. From somebody else it might have sounded sarcastic, but not from him; he was sincere.

"The girls have the whole state behind them, but that don't mean a thing if they don't get support from their own family. That's what counts." The wisdom of Mrs. Melli. She summoned Yvonne to visit all the way over to Barrington the day after Easter. "I'll feed you a cup of coffee. Maybe you want tea, tea's better for you."

A long trafficky rainy ride. "It's easy to find my house, right off Route 103," she had said, but Yvonne had to go back and forth on 103 twice before she found it, an oversized brick ranch house painted white. It was the day after Easter, but on a tree in the front yard, they still had Christmas lights hung up in the shape of a cross. And there was still tinfoil on the door. "When it gets warm I take it down. Don't let him scare you." An immense black dog was close enough to bite. Mrs. Melli hitched her hand under its collar and began pulling it away. "I can smell it, I always smell a winner, I figured you'd cream the rest of the girls from Rhode Island." She pushed the dog behind a door and closed it with a bang. "Shut up, you stupid dog! His name is John Kennedy. We're Republicans."

Yvonne didn't know where to put her jacket. She left it on.

"Are you certain you're going to win?" Mrs. Melli was short and dark-haired, with a sharp nose, a sharp chin. "Do you really believe it?" She sat down on the sofa and patted it to make Yvonne come sit beside her.

"Well, I can't be certain."

"Then you're going to lose." Mrs. Melli picked up a yellow teacup, English bone china. "I'll give you sugar if you want it, but no cookies here, no cakes. When I ask you for tea, that's what I mean, just tea." There was a silver tea set on the table in front of the sofa, actually silverplate, Gorham. Yvonne's mother had one just like it at home. "But no little cookies, no cake! I've seen them put on weight, five pounds right before the pageant, stupid."

"Well, I don't think I'm going to lose either."

"If you're not sure you're going to win, you might just as well skip the pageant. Don't go, stay home, sugar."

"Sugar." Yvonne balanced the cup on her knees, the winning right knee. The table was so close to the sofa there was no room for her to cross her legs. "What would happen if I didn't go?"

Mrs. Melli put down the teapot and turned around to stare angrily at Yvonne. "Trouble." From behind the closed door, the dog started barking again, maybe there were two dogs. "Somebody else on the committee said it, I didn't say it, but they were right." To compete with the dogs, her voice got louder. "You take a Wellesley girl, some smarty girl from the Ivy League, you got trouble because they think they're better than the pageant."

"I don't feel I'm better than the pageant."

"You're not."

"I was just curious." For comfort Yvonne started fiddling with her necklace, her favorite one, the little Y on a gold chain.

"You go to Wellesley, you figure it out. We send in the runner-up." The dog had quieted. Mrs. Melli was still loud. "That colored girl. And if we do, don't think it would be so awful, we'd have the only colored in there, so we'd be sure to place in the top ten. She's a good singer that colored girl, she's very musical, you want to back out?"

"I don't want to back out. Why should I back out? But I'm not going to kid myself and believe I'm going to win. I'll do the best I can, that's all."

"You poor thing!" Mrs. Melli put her hand on

Yvonne's arm. "I'm not being fair. It's just the strain. They all get nervous waiting for the pageant, everybody looking at them all the time and telling them what to do. You just relax, I'm pushing too hard. Just be yourself, that's the best way. That's what they want from you anyway."

The dog started growling.

"John Kennedy's unhappy." Yvonne let go of her necklace.

"That's the other one, Jackie, don't let her scare you. I'm pushing too hard. You know why? Because I'm so competitive, I want to come in first. You may not feel that way."

"I want to come in first. But I wonder if I can, fifty girls, I mean they're all going to be pretty girls."

"You just listen to me, you'll win."

Did she say that every year? Or did she wait till she got the right girl and then say it? Mrs. Melli suddenly reached down beside the sofa. "See this?" She pulled up a copy of *Vogue* magazine. "Toilet paper! You don't want clothes from here. Denim! I bet some stupid girl shows up in a gown made out of it. What do you like best, satin or net?"

The wrong answer would be the sign of a loser.

"I might look better in satin."

"But what do you like best?"

"It depends on the gown."

"You've got to wear either red or white. I noticed it, the girl who wins she always wears red or white. But that's only Swimsuit. On the gown satin could be O.K. But not too suggestive."

"I'm not wearing satin."

"I thought you liked it."

"I'll look at the gown first, then I'll decide. I'll pick out the gown, not the material."

"You mean you don't want to sew it." Mrs. Melli poured herself another cup of tea, ominously, without offering any to Yvonne.

"I don't like to sew."

"I'll help you, I got a pattern book. I'm good sewing. I made that slipcover over there, would you know it. I made the Christmas-tree skirt, it's all shirred. Felt. That's not easy to sew, right?"

"I'm going to buy it."

"You lose points, you don't sew it. Don't you want to win?"

Maybe she didn't.

"I'll shop in Boston, Bonwit Teller, I could never sew as good as that."

"With me helping you can. I'll go shopping with you. Don't dare get it alone, I'll kill you if you do."

But was it proper for Miss Rhode Island to appear in a gown purchased in Boston?

"Don't worry about it." Her mother, ironing a linen skirt for Yvonne to take back to Wellesley, comforted her. "They all come from New York originally anyway."

"Maybe the fabric was woven in Rhode Island, that's possible, it's still a big textile state." One of Miss Rhode Island's gifts had been a book about the state. "But not as big as it used to be." Yvonne pinned the skirt onto a hanger. She didn't have to wrinkle it in a suitcase. It could hang in the car while she was being driven back to Wellesley.

An out-of-state school.

Another danger.

Her father worked out of state. In Attleboro, Massa-

81

chusetts. She had relatives out of state. In Fall River. She spent most of her time out of state. Miss Massachusetts was, perhaps, prettier, more poised. She could see George Kirby atop Miss Massachusetts on the floor, on the shag rug in his apartment on Beacon Street in Boston. Miss Massachusetts would win, Yvonne would lose, she would be eliminated in the first round, Miss Rhode Island usually was. Miss Mississippi won, Miss South Carolina, Miss Minnesota. Does not a Jew have feelings? She could see the harbor out of her bedroom window, she could see Conanicut, the island where Conanicus the noble Indian made peace with Roger Williams, the noble white man. She could see above it the gray pearly light, Rhode Island light; but it was the same in Massachusetts when the sky was overcast, it was more like that in Massachusetts, there was more light there, more land, more trees, more leaves, more stones, more people, more women. Were there bigger breasts? She could see farther, across to the island called Rhode Island, to the town of Portsmouth, two bridges away: islands, bridges, breakwaters, lighthouses, she represented the Ocean State. They had more land, she had more ocean. A mermaid, a Nausicaä waiting for a weary Odysseus to sail into her harbor. But of course, during Easter vacation, two weeks of it, she could only get in touch with Truston once discreetly. They couldn't telephone each other at home, it wasn't fair.

VI

They have discovered this statistically: The more beautiful one is, the more one is loved.

But they have also discovered this: The more beautiful one is, the more one is hated.

"I don't hate you, not one bit," Joseph said before she went back to Wellesley from vacation. "I love you. You're my sister."

"How could we hate our little girl?" There is no hatred in a parent's heart, there is no hatred in a lover's, and as for a just plain date, even Fino, as for a roommate, as for a classmate, they cannot hate her, they don't know her well enough. Mrs. Melli, even you do not know her, you will never know her. Can you ever know any of them, the beautiful?

Fool, do not hate her. For then you are in her power.

Brown University, Departments of Sociology, Psychology, History, Classics—their findings: Look and die. Do not look on her, avert your gaze. Truston daringly stands her in front of him, he begins to unbutton her blouse, the top button, looking her in the eyes. The light is on in the motel, the three-way lamp, light shining through the sand-colored shade, reflecting off the glass atop the dresser, enclosing the rows of the chenille bedspread. As each button opens light reaches her breasts, the bra is off, he looks. Oh, God, if I could only look, I wouldn't care if I were struck dead.

Truston, do you dare?

"Everybody wants to look, but you're the only one I let look, Truston, treat me nice."

How nice can he treat her? There is no way.

"You treat me nice, I'm the one who needs it."

He looks, he looks, he shuts his eyes, they would burn out. He would turn to glass, to ash, the dried seaweed on Moonstone, his hair burned by the sun, his body turned to sand.

"Look at me!"

Her insistent voice, what place is it coming from?

"I like it with my eyes shut."

"It's not nice if you don't look at me." Under him, uneasy movement, shifting his heavy body along with her own.

"I looked at you before."

"I thought you wanted to look at me."

Oh, Truston, you have been killed.

As if he could ever control her. Therefore, she controls him. But what could he do, break her other arm? I will pierce his heart with my blades, all of them. On the white ice, blood.

"You are going to win, I can tell it, I can see it." Both her thighs were grasped tight in his hands.

"Don't leave a mark."

"I'm going to leave a mark on you somewhere."

"Not where it will show."

With a knife? With a gun? So that all the other men will see it in the future, God will see it on the last day, the undertaker, everyone will know. Maybe his initials, TC;

84

maybe just his name, Truston. Maybe it was worth it, she would never be in a nude movie, never be a foldout.

Starting out with a little nibble, his teeth just below the place that would show if she wore a string bikini. What was he writing with his tongue? This word: Mine.

"I do love him, I never imagined I'd have an affair like this." Marilyn was walking alongside her to the one class they were taking together, Introduction to Art. "I never imagined I'd have an involvement with an older man, a married man, I always just dated before, you know, boys."

"I have already, but only in Europe." Unlike Yvonne, Marilyn had really seen the Primavera, the Venus de Milo. "An Austrian, at a hotel. But only a week and I didn't tell him my real name."

"Then it wasn't much of an involvement."

"It wasn't so different. Do you know what he called me? Miss America, because he knew I was American. Sometimes he called me the Statue of Liberty. He said he liked big women."

"I think I'm really in love." Inside Yvonne's mouth her tongue moved up and down, as his had.

"Have you told him?"

"I would never do that."

"Why not? He'd like to hear it."

"I have to wait for him first, he's never said it."

A lie.

He had said it. His hands full of her, his hips pushing, his mouth at her neck, that's what he said, not whispering it the way he should, but rushing the words out bodily. Clearly it wasn't her he loved, but something else. There in the motel in the night—could Miss Massachusetts hear it? it was in her territory—with the motel sign, VACANCY,

85

VACANCY, flashing on and off while the words spurted out of him: Miss America, I love you.

The circle, exactly three times Yvonne's height.
The shoulders, pressed down.
The arms, extended at heart level.
The hands, gracefully free. Never clenched.
"Show me." Truston made her stand up on the motel rug next to the bed. "Which leg do you raise up?"
The left. Yvonne raised it, she leaned her head forward, she spread her arms out, palms facing the floor. "It's a strain. You can't do it very well without skates."
"You have to smile more. More real."
"It's hard enough to keep the position."
A tickle would make her smile.
She smiled.
But at the rink, Truston wasn't there, he was sitting at his law desk, would he run for President someday, first he had to be the senator from Rhode Island. But who are we kidding? Does even a senator from Rhode Island stand a chance nationally? If the Kennedys came from Rhode Island, they would have been nowhere.
A perfect circle, three times her height. All on the right foot. The proper edge held. Held the second time around. Held the third time too. All of her body leaning slightly into the circle.
She would not be judged on a perfectly skated circle, though. The circle of the nipple, the circle of the breast, the circle at the center of the eye, those were more important.
"You make me go round and round," Truston said. And he did with his finger, round and round, lightly tracing one breast and then the other.
The world is turning. How much queenship is left? To

86

do a one-foot spin, start with a figure three. Hands locked in position, moved out a little, around and around, the head turns, the eyes kept wide open, don't shut them, it makes you dizzier, each point on the shoulder, each atom of the blade spinning in its circles, thousands of circles spin, heel pressed into the ice for speed, spinning.

Once when he was inside, on top of her, Yvonne said, "You make me dizzy."

"I don't want to be hurting you."

"No, the idea makes me dizzy, it all makes me dizzy, I feel I'm going around in circles like when I was a little girl, I used to spin around and my father used to catch me. I used to practice spinning."

Practice, that's the answer.

"The girls who win, they keep practicing their talent, they keep practicing the walk down the runway. You need a little practice with your makeup. You got to get that little extra curve on the lower lip. Here, let me show you," and when Mrs. Melli touched the lipstick brush to Yvonne's lips, the two great sleek dogs, sick with desire, started barking again hopelessly. But the chief practice is this, the practice of Truston. Practice in bed. Even Mrs. Melli might agree.

It can't be a minus. It has to add something.

It builds a girl up. It increases confidence.

It helps a girl understand what it's all about.

Do you think any harm could possibly come from hearing:

"Yvonne, please come close to me. Oh, Yvonne, you are my darling. Yvonne, I really love you, I have to say it."

Every girl ought to hear it.

Three times a day.

And she ought to believe it.

Believe it, you are the only one for me, the other one she is an illusion.

Believe me, you are the girl I have seen since I was a child, going down the hill to the waterfront, over the water, it is you. And if you think I love you only because you are beautiful, Yvonne, only because you are famous, only because you are the one woman in Rhode Island who is worthy to stand atop the great dome with the perfect man, held in his granite arms, even if you are this rare, that cannot explain my love for you; because I came to love you as I pushed out of the first channel and I will love you when I go down to the final home, I loved you when I first went into the bay, running into the terrifying waves, running from them, but then back again, always into, until finally I immersed myself, and that is how I immerse myself in love for you, Yvonne.

Yvonne, if you doubt me, then place a mark on me, cut my skin. If you doubt me put a scarlet letter T on my cheeks, T for traitor, T the letter that looks like a man. If you doubt me, cut it with this knife, on my back, on my forehead. Oh, T for traitor, Y for Yvonne, V for victory. I come to you, Yvonne, to the Y, to the V atop it, the cleft letter.

This is Y.

Y. I straddle its limbs, I climb out on each one to its end, I kiss its sweet edge, I tongue it. And, at the center, the triangle, inverted, with its ecstatic angles! Into and around each one I go, grasping the raised limbs of the Y, pushing them outward to dive forward, into the insatiable space between them, you, Yvonne.

T for Truston. Feel it, it is the letter of the man, put your hand around it. I will write it inside you, inside your mouth, I have written it inside you, I have written it on your skin in every place, I know it is there.

V is the letter for victory, T is the letter for trophy.

T, press it on my skin a hundred times.

Here, under my breast.

Here, where my thighs rub together in this place to form a Y.

I don't care, I don't care if I win, what is winning, why should I care, what I care for is this. This T, every part of it. It is different every time, it is beautiful. T. Do you think I'm no good, not physically, I don't mean that, you know what I mean. If that's what you thought, if you thought I was only a cheap Frenchie, if you thought I was a quick lay, just nothing, just Miss Rhode Island, only that, just a pair of tits, just a pretty ass, I'd jump off the bridge into the bay, I'd drive the car, gun it right down to the floor and into the bay, you can do that when you're going sixty, if that's what you thought, if all you care about is once a week, Tuesday night, get it off, look what I got, little Miss America, aren't I the terrific one, I laid her, if that's what you thought.

"Who's your boyfriend?" Mrs. Melli had come up to Boston to take Yvonne out shopping, to show her the sort of clothes she shouldn't buy.

First stop Bonwit Teller. In her hand Mrs. Melli held the pamphlet sent out by the pageant people in Atlantic City, the official guide for contestants. Yvonne already had a copy, but she kept that at home. It wasn't something to be brought to Wellesley for other girls to see. "Your personal taste will help dictate the selection of your wardrobe; however do not discount the good advice from 'someone in the know.' " Standing next to the brightly colored bathing suits hanging on the rack, Mrs. Melli read to her from the pamphlet. "That's me, I'm the someone in the know they're talking about. It's your money, it's your figure, and like it says you can help dictate the selection. Oh, that's pretty."

Yvonne had picked out a bathing suit. One-piece, that was regulation. Bronze-colored. "Too low-cut in back," she said. "I don't think I can wear it."

"You can get away with it. So what if it isn't red."

"I thought it wasn't supposed to be low-cut in back."

Mrs. Melli consulted her brochure. "Would you call that back plunging?"

"I'll try it on."

But when Yvonne came out of the fitting room she was fully dressed.

"What the hell happened?"

"It had a plunging back, I could see."

"Next time, you show me. Don't judge it yourself. You got eyes in the back of your head?"

"I'm not blind, there was a mirror."

"You show me next time. Here, you try this on. And you show me or do you want me to come in there with you?"

To see if Yvonne was a virgin? To inspect the little cherry-colored hickeys with which Truston had adorned her hips.

"I'll come out. You sit here and rest. You look tired."

"I don't get tired."

Was Mrs. Melli gaining dominance over her?

"Who's your boyfriend?" Mrs. Melli tried again later when they were having tea in the Ritz Carlton. Tea, that's what Mrs. Melli said, but she ordered a vodka and tonic. "Go ahead, you have something too, I'm not a monster. You need to relax too sometimes. I think you're a little

90

tense. Sometimes I worry, you're going to be too uptight when you get to Atlantic City, that's one of the disadvantages of choosing a Wellesley girl."

"I'll have a Coke right now. I have an exam I have to study for. If I drink, I won't study tonight."

"I bet you're drinking Coke so you can smoke marijuana. I know the ones who don't drink liquor do that."

"I like Coke. I'm American, Miss America, that's why I like Coke. Maybe it helps, maybe they score you on that. Don't you want me to have a Coke?"

"Get her a Coke," Mrs. Melli said to the waitress. She patted Yvonne's hand. "You ever smoke marijuana?"

"No." It was apparent Yvonne was lying.

"How do you feel about marijuana?"

"You go to parties, they're all smoking it, I don't like the smell. I don't like smoking, period. It pollutes the atmosphere."

"You tell that to the judges. But tell them you tried it once, hear that? Just once, just to try it and you didn't like it. Who's your boyfriend?"

"I don't have a boyfriend right now."

"Well, you need one."

"I get along fine as it is."

"I wish my son was here, he'd eat you up. He likes them pretty like you. But he's out on the West Coast, thirty-one years old."

Yvonne D. Melli! What to do until the Coca-Cola comes? Make conversation? About what? "This is such a nice hotel, I understand it's the best hotel in Boston, I've never been here before. I've never stayed in a hotel in Boston. I never stayed in a hotel anywhere, just motels. That's one thing I'm looking forward to in Atlantic City. What's the name of the hotel I stay in?"

"Haddon. They're going to ask you do you have a

boyfriend, what will you say then? I never had one with-out a boyfriend before. They all have boyfriends."

"Maybe I'll have a boyfriend by then."

"You ever had a boyfriend?"

Most popular, most beautiful. Most humiliated. "Of course I have."

"Maybe you can get him back until September? Why don't you invite him to a dance? Don't they have dances at Wellesley, daisy chains, that kind of thing? Don't they have proms?"

"The last boyfriend I had was the one who tripped me up skating."

This time it was Mrs. Melli who changed the subject. "We should go to Filene's next."

"Remember this," she said after the waitress had served the drinks, "your greatest competition is yourself. That's very important, that's a basic key thing, and if you forget it, you're sunk."

Suddenly Yvonne's hands felt cold. The ice in her drink was melting. Tears ran down the outside of the glass. "Is that what you mean? I'm going to lose? Do you mean I'm arranging for myself to lose?"

"What are you talking about? That's what it says in the pageant guidelines: 'Your greatest competition is your-self.' See, it's right here." She pushed through the pages and there it was, underlined. "Your greatest competitor is yourself."

But Yvonne still didn't know exactly what it meant.

"I've got your number," Mrs. Melli said as they were walking across Boston Common toward Filene's. "You don't really want to win. You'd be embarrassed to win. Maybe you're not relaxed about your own body, you know what I mean? For some women it's a terrible prob-lem once they get married."

"I don't have that kind of problem. I don't want to not win." In the thin air of outdoors, Yvonne's voice seemed diminished. "I don't want to be a loser."

"It's that or win, kid, you can't do both." Mrs. Melli sounded more than usually impatient.

"Listen, I'm going to do my best, I'm going to try my hardest, but it's scary, everybody is depending on me, the whole state, and they're not depending on my brain —listen, I might as well just say the truth—all they're depending is my tits. It's embarrassing, how can you be relaxed about that? You'd be embarrassed too, you were never in this position, you don't know how dirty their minds are, you gloss it over, good manners, good taste, intelligence, talent—all that stuff in the brochure." She snapped her fingers against Mrs. Melli's pocketbook, where the brochure lay. "It's tits. I'm not that big a feminist, but it's obvious what it's all about. They don't have an Old Lady America contest, they should have one for old ladies. Before I die, I'll start it."

"Now, Yvonne, you're getting out of control."

True, her eyes were becoming red, her voice was getting nasal. They were shrill like a mother and daughter together on a shopping expedition. Yvonne's chest felt heavy, those boobs, they weighed her down, she wanted to sink into the earth, into the Common, Massachusetts earth, not even her own. "I'm getting out of control, right? Why should I be controlled by this travesty?"

"You didn't have to get into it."

"I did, I did, and it's not that I don't like it. But they hate me, everybody hates me because I'm pretty. I thought they'd like me." Yvonne suddenly sat down on a bench. "What a surprise!"

"I don't hate you." Mrs. Melli sat down too.

It was true. Mrs. Melli didn't hate her.

"So long as I do what you want me to do."

"That's my job. You can't blame me for doing my job, can you?"

The bench was old and splintery. But it faced south. Yvonne didn't have to look at the dome of the Massachusetts State House.

"Sometimes I just want to cut out. Canada, France, anywhere just to get away from this."

"Here," Mrs. Melli said. She had taken a Kleenex out of her pocketbook for Yvonne.

"You think the only thing the men want out of me is 'good manners, good taste, good sportsmanship'? A piece of ass, that's what they want. No, that's wrong, they don't even want that. They tell themselves it's what they want, maybe that's why they go after me, but that's not what they want. They want to screw Miss Rhode Island, that's what they want, it isn't even about me, it isn't about women even. It's about men."

The cry of Anne Hutchinson beside this Common, the accusation, the shriek "Wherefore?"—it was no louder. Her they sent off into the wilderness. Yvonne they pushed out onto a runway.

"Come on, Yvonne, you got to grin and bear it." Mrs. Melli patted her hand.

Suddenly it was apparent. Each year Mrs. Melli had a talk like this, maybe twice a year, maybe three times, with the chosen queen.

"Did you ever hear anyone say this before?"

"Never, all the girls get upset, but always in a different way. Don't worry about it."

"I've got a boyfriend."

"Why didn't you say so?"

"He's forty-four years old."

Mrs. Melli got up and started walking away. "If any-

94

body finds out"—she turned around to Yvonne but kept walking—"if anybody finds out, I'll murder you."

"He wants me to win." Yvonne had to stand up and follow her.

"Of course he does, stupid. You don't have to go to Wellesley to figure that out." Mrs. Melli was walking fast. "Ninety-nine percent stupid. What the hell do I get out of this? I don't have to be in it. Listen, Yvonne, you better break it off. Right now. Call him up, here's a dime." She snapped open her pocketbook.

"I don't want to break it off." Yvonne pulled on Mrs. Melli's arm. "I think I love him."

"What the hell does that have to do with it? You got a responsibility, you took it on, nobody else did. Now look what you're doing."

"He's helping me do better." Mrs. Melli shook Yvonne's arm away. "He wants me to win."

"Do you think Miss America is sleeping with some old fart?"

"How do I know what Miss America's doing?"

"You're never going to know. I should call Atlantic City, let them know what's going on. I never had one like this before. This is a new one on me. You might have just talked yourself out of it. I bet that's what you had in mind all the time anyway but won't Mr. Handsome be disappointed. He thought he had it and now it's all slipping through his fingers. What a laugh! He deserves it."

"That wouldn't matter to Truston!" A lie.

"What's his name, Rusty?"

"Forget it."

"I don't care what his name is, you're throwing yourself away on him." They had reached the edge of the Common. A traffic light flashed the green word WALK. "Come on, stupid, Filene's is down this street. You think he'd stick with you if you don't win the pageant? Well, maybe he will. They hold on until you're too old to get married, then they let go when you really start needing them. He's married, right?"

"That's completely unfair."

"Does your mother and father know about him?"

"It's none of their business." Behind her back Yvonne could hear the sound of cars gunning their way down the street. The light must have changed.

"You better not tell, your father would pull out the knife on him, that's what my father would have done. I never had a daughter, but I know my husband would do it."

"Maybe you can forget about my boyfriend." Yvonne stopped. She grabbed Mrs. Melli's arm again, she turned and looked her directly in the eyes. "Don't think about it, it's something private. I'm sorry I told you."

But Mrs. Melli wasn't having any. "Come on! Come on!" She didn't stop walking. "Never mind that. He's going to be watching you on TV. Let's hope he gets to see something of you. You know, if you aren't in the finals, the semis, you don't get much exposure, they always hurry over Rhode Island anyway."

"I don't want to talk about him."

"I already dropped the subject, you won't hear about it from me. As far as I'm concerned, he's dead. It's no skin off my back, you want to fool around, that's up to you. I got a better picture of you, that's what counts." They were crossing the street in front of Filene's. "Let's go to the third floor. I only wish you satisfied easy with bathing suits like you do with a man. That's all."

"I told her, I told Mrs. Melli." Yvonne confessed it to Truston. She was lying down on her stomach, her breasts were hidden, her legs were held close together. But she did have her hand on his arm, she was touching him, the hairy skin of his arm, not quite as hairy as Poulos's, though.

"What did you tell her? You don't want to win? You confessed it."

"You think like her a little bit, maybe you ought to go to bed with her." Yvonne moved her hand away, slightly. "I told her about us."

"Did you tell her my name?"

"No." Was Truston disappointed? "But I'm sure she'll ask sometime."

Truston didn't say: Don't tell her. He put his arm around Yvonne. "Now she knows. Now Julie—that's your roommate, right?—she knows and a couple of the other girls, right?"

"They may have told someone, I don't know, I told them not to."

"You're playing with fire, don't let anyone find out. You'll really be in trouble. They could bounce you."

"What about you, you could be in trouble too. Have you told anyone? What about that?"

The answer: a kiss.

"Come on, Truston, answer the question."

Another kiss. Love will find a way. That's what the song says. Enough kissing would make anyone forget the questions; it would make me forget my questions, one two three. Enough of that would make me forget. You too, don't deny it.

"Did you tell your wife?"

Truston moved over so that he was lying on top of Yvonne. "What kind of a question is that?" he said. He began nibbling at the back of her neck.

She didn't shake him off. That was his answer.

What kind of an answer is that?

VII

One, an actress living in Hollywood. Bit parts, also commercials.

One, an inspector at a factory making pens and pencils.

One, a nursery-school teacher.

One, a governor's wife. Oh, Truston, all the time pushing forward, but you never ran for office.

One, a dancer with a ballet company in Europe.

One, a piano teacher. Also a model.

One, a social worker.

And one, a Latin professor, the mother of Rhode Islanders. Rise up, boys, face forward, girls! Construe!

"The best thing I could do in life would be to become a Latin professor, that's what I really want, that and children. But I don't want to talk to you about that, we're never going to get married."

"You don't have to stay in Rhode Island, you should get to New York, California. It's a dead language, you're too alive for that." Truston put a hand on her belly. "This is a good chance for you to get out. You should use it."

"Why didn't you leave?" The body, just as it says in the sex manuals, is an incredibly subtle instrument. Just hold your breath, recede a sixteenth of an inch, tighten your arms, and his hand slides away.

"I'm talking about you, not me."

"Well, let's talk about you. Why push me, if you didn't push yourself to do it? I like Rhode Island. I want to marry some boy and settle down here. I wouldn't mind living in Wickford. Do you think I was lying to the judges? I meant it, I want to stay . . ."

"You're foolish. You'll miss your whole life."

"I'm having it now." In bed. "You're not my father, you're my lover." Proof: Yvonne tweaked him, in the right place. "Remember, this is supposed to be the most memorable year of my life."

"If you stay in Rhode Island, you could get stuck with me all your life." Truston whispered the words.

"Oh, Truston, is that a proposal?" Yvonne sat up on the bed.

Exposed: the breasts of the beautiful mistress.

"Maybe it's a proposition."

Another tweak. This one not so cheerful, a little harder. Almost so it hurt.

"That's not very nice."

Modest maidens do not touch a man like that, most-likely-to-succeed girls, beauty queens, Miss Rhode Islands. They move their hands gently and slowly over one body, their own, when they are alone, and over other bodies at appropriate times. They do not tweak.

"Sometimes," Truston said, "maybe I'm not a very nice person."

"Well, I am." Yvonne was over him, he was still lying down, looking up at her. "All the time. I'd never be your girlfriend if it weren't for Miss Rhode Island. If I weren't in college, if I were out in the world, I'd steer clear of a married man, let me tell you."

He sat up; he put his arm around her shoulders; he began stroking her neck; he began playing with her ear.

"I mean, it's fine for now, it's easier than with a boy in college, all the time bragging, 'I'm Miss Rhode Island's boyfriend,' all that stuff. That's why I didn't like Donny Fino, not because he broke my arm. Even if he hadn't broken my arm, I wouldn't have gone out with him much more. Too braggy. You might be bragging too, but I don't have to know it. With you I'm in isolation, sort of."

His hand on her neck, her ear, motionless, heavy, as if paralyzed.

"I mean, we don't have a future, Truston. You can't imagine we would, no matter how much I care for you."

His hand started moving again.

"Mrs. Melli thinks I'm wrong to be sleeping with you. But it's right, it's the right thing to do. I'm not a virgin, it hasn't been that many. But I wanted to go to bed with you."

"Are you sorry?"

"You're like self-protection. It's not like with a date. I don't always have to show off."

"I think you're snobby. That's why you like me. You're a little Canuck."

True, his accent was often rounder, richer than hers.

"I want to meet some of your friends sometime." He took her head in his hands and turned her toward him, so she would have to look him in the eyes. "You've seen my friends, when we met. You've seen my house."

"Why don't you come down to Atlantic City? Lots of people are coming."

"No, I want to meet your friends. This Julie, Marilyn, the ones you talk about. Maybe sometime they can join us for dinner."

100

"Aren't I enough?"

"It doesn't take anything away from you. It adds to you." Not only Miss Rhode Island, Miss Rhode Island's maids-in-waiting. A glutton.

"I don't want them to meet you. I don't want you to get near them, I don't think you should ever see them, you shouldn't be so piggy." A smile, a soft kiss on Truston's cheek. Would a selfish person kiss like that? A cruel person? A reserved person? "I think your mind's too imaginative as it is."

Pictures.

Kneel on the floor, feet close together; lean your head back; arch. The letter C.

"Don't you get tired of those silly exercises?" Now everything Julie said to Yvonne had an edge of anger. Of jealousy? Let's hope so.

"Stop picking on me. Just because I'm Miss Rhode Island."

"You keep thinking everything is about Miss Rhode Island. It isn't. You've changed. You know when you changed, when you started seeing Truston. You changed a lot. You ought to go out with some other boys."

Another arch.

The head touched the floor, the breasts receded, the thighs spread back, the little mound could be seen beneath the leotard. "I don't want to see anybody else."

"Some new face, that's what you need." Julie herself had just gone out with a medical student named Paul Gold. "You should try Paul's friend Pritchett, he's nice, he's a medical student."

Medical students have seen the body.

"Come to a party, they have parties all the time in this apartment on the Fenway. Marilyn took me, they want

101

lots of different girls. You'd be the hit of the evening."

"I don't want to go out, everybody looks at me, Miss Rhode Island."

"That's what it's about."

"I'll just wait this year out, after the pageant, I won't have to worry then. They'll make me smoke grass."

"Is that why you won't go out?" Julie sounded shocked. "Miss Rhode Island can't smoke grass?"

"I'm in love with Truston."

"Before you met Truston you weren't really going out."

"Well, now there's no reason to. You should meet him, you come meet him, you'll like him. Why don't you come out to dinner with us this week?"

"I don't want to meet him. You should go out on some normal dates. He's just exploiting you."

The answer, quickly: another arch.

"You laugh at this exercise, but it's the best one, it thins out the belly. You could use it."

"I'll do it if you come to one of Marilyn's parties."

"O.K., I'll go."

Whose capitulation? Julie scrambled down to the floor.

Two girls, the double arch, bellies up facing the heavens.

"No, you kneel, get your legs under yourself."

"I need work on my thighs."

"I can show you one for that too." Yvonne's arch was perfect. "Lift up, lift up, lift up, lift up," she whispered happily until beside her Julie was arched too.

An aged apartment on the Fenway, up four flights of stairs. The walls were cracked, painted yellow. The curtains had probably been there, lease after lease, for twenty years, faded, a grayed-out yellow.

"How can doctors live with such dirt?" Yvonne had to ask Marilyn. Julie, inexplicably, had decided not to come.

"They have to be antiseptic. I guess this is a relief. He's good-looking, so I forget about it. The sheets are clean anyway. Besides, we don't eat here."

All those boys, one hand holding a cigarette, the other hand wandering up and down a girl's back, squeezing her shoulder gently; but they are talking to each other.

"You'll have fun. Are you really having fun?"

There was no answer. The walls looked sad, darkened, the color of the eyes of the girls who were still searching for partners. There was, Yvonne could see it, dust on the brass lamp beside the sofa.

But listen to what Marilyn says. She knows. "It's all right for fun, Yvonne. I've enjoyed it myself for fun and with someone who, if I told you his name, you'd recognize it. It's a show-business name, and the public thinks he's got such a marvelous family life too. But you have to take care of yourself too. I never stopped going out with other boys, this was last summer. It never kept me away from parties, and you know why?" This was the wisdom of New York. "You don't have to give up anything you don't want to, not a damn thing, especially if you're a beauty queen. Do you think any of those movie stars have to put out? Of course not, they pick and choose. They do what they want, and that's it."

On a table in the corner, two jugs of wine, one red, one white. Plastic cups. The apartment didn't have a view of the Fenway. It faced back, away from the park. So what! It smelled of grass anyway.

Standing by the window next to another boy equally

tall: Poulos. Suddenly visible. He was wearing his white medical-school coat.

"I know him." Yvonne grabbed Marilyn's arm, she pointed to the white coat. "Arthur Poulos."

"My God!" Marilyn said.

No wonder! Poulos appeared even better-looking than he had in the past.

"I told you to come. I was right. Julie was right."

"Sh," Yvonne whispered. "Sh." But she was at the party, she was there. "Sh, don't let him hear you."

Behind the white coat, a black window. Poulos turned toward them, so did the man he was talking to, the two of them swiveling around, coming toward. Poulos smiled; a Rhode Islander, he knew the queen. Arise, Sir Arthur, would it be King Arthur? It almost was once in the past, practically, three summers ago in Rhode Island. But now would he kneel down before her? Would he march up to her and kiss her toes, those pink-painted toes beneath soft leather?

Keep still, Yvonne! Time is unreeling.

The portion of Poulos is to come forward and kneel down before her, to beg for a touch.

The portion of Yvonne is to stand over him. She is wearing a long gown, she is wearing a golden chain for a belt and on the end of the chain, hanging, a golden coin of Isabella the Queen, the queen responsible for America.

The portions of Marilyn, of Poulos's friend: to stand on either side of them echoing every motion.

Kneel, Poulos! In the middle of the party. Everyone turned around to look.

"What are you kneeling for?"

"You're the queen of Rhode Island. I'm a Rhode Islander."

"Oh, come off it, Arthur! Don't make such a show."

Everybody was looking. Even the people slouched on the sofa, or leaning against it, sitting on the floor smoking grass.

One of them began applauding.

"Get up, you'll get your pants dirty down there."

"You'll have to give me permission."

Poulos's friend knelt down in front of Marilyn.

It was to laugh.

Two or three people started applauding.

"Women's lib," someone called through the smoke; and then someone else, a girl, began hissing.

"I'm not giving mine permission to get up." Marilyn's teeth seemed to be longer, her face and her hips broader.

"Jesus, Marilyn, I told you I shouldn't have come." There were no empty seats. Only one solution. Yvonne took it. She sat down on the floor next to where Poulos was kneeling. "Would you get me a drink?" she said politely.

Someone handed by a joint.

Poulos took a hit of it.

He handed it to Yvonne.

"Would you please get me a drink of wine? How about you?" Marilyn was still standing. "Will you get me a drink?"

Marilyn took the joint instead.

Poulos sprang up to get her a drink. Grass, wine, he leaped up like an athlete.

"I always loved you," he said when he came back. "And when I saw that write-up about you in the paper, you were chosen Miss Rhode Island, I knew I was right."

"All you wanted was to make it with me. That's what you kept telling me all the time."

It was true. "I go wild whenever I touch you." Three

105

years ago Poulos had said it. "I spend all my time thinking about it. I can't study. I stop caring if I'm going to get into medical school. It makes my mouth dry out. Then wet again, then dry. There's a connection in men." Nerves connecting the salivary glands with the stirring in the place where the balls hang beside the inside of the thighs.

"I still feel it now. You like red wine, right? I always felt it." Before she even became Miss Rhode Island, before she was even voted Most Beautiful Senior, long before she could become Miss America, if she ever did become it.

As if shot, shazam-O, by a bolt from heaven.

Where did the bolt hit her? Once Poulos had dared to ask her. Between the soft legs? Was it hitting her all the time?

Admittedly. He was better-looking than Truston ever had been. He was taller, he wasn't so solidly built, but he wasn't delicate-boned either, like Fino. He had black hairs visible on the back of his wrist, coming out of his collar, he would never trip her up skating. Was he the only man around who wanted her, not because she was Miss Rhode Island, not because she was pretty, not because she had personality, but because she would let him touch her, she would touch back, she was warm to the touch. It was a relief. She was replaceable by another woman.

"I never drink anything more than wine when I smoke." He sat down next to her. His knee touched her thigh.

"I used to smoke. I stopped smoking. I never really liked to, anyway. It makes my throat hurt."

"When did you stop?"

"As soon as I became Miss Rhode Island. Miss Rhode Island can't get high, Miss America; they'd die if they caught me. I wasn't going to get into that position. I don't even like it here. It's obvious, the smell. If I get caught now there'd be trouble."

"Nobody's going to catch you."

"They're just waiting for something like this. The cops could come." A plot. The net is getting tighter. The crime is here. Someone passed another joint to Poulos. He took an energetic hit, deep, zealous, and then, his voice unnaturally deepened by the smoke, masculine, deep inside, handed it to her. One baleful word: "Here."

It could make her again like other women.

"No way! I don't want it." This could be it, the end, Miss Rhode Island destroyed. Her throat was constricting, her mouth was dry. She could see the tears in Mrs. Melli's eyes. We almost had a winner, but she blew it, she let it go up in smoke.

Marilyn reached over and took the joint. One drag and then she put it in front of Yvonne's mouth. "Come on, one for Mommy."

"None for me."

"What are you afraid of?" A girl Yvonne didn't know, watching, shouted it from the other side of the room.

"Who's that? What business is it of hers? Do I have to be on public display every time I go out?" She pushed Marilyn's hand away angrily. "I said it, no! You know what prize they ought to give in the pageant?" Poulos didn't know, Marilyn didn't know. "A free psychoanalysis! You have to be crazy to get into it. All my motives must have been bad ones."

"Don't be such a little girl." Marilyn was still holding on to the joint.

"Well, I can't smoke."

"You can smoke." Poulos wasn't letting her be Miss Rhode Island. "You just can't get caught smoking."

Yvonne Doucette, Miss Rhode Island, shown here surrendering her crown after Boston police yesterday caught her in possession of marijuana. On her left, Marilyn. On her right, Poulos.

"I won't do it. I want to get out of here. Let's go swimming. Let's go out to some beach. Never mind the grass, let's do something else. I don't care if it's a little cool. So we catch pneumonia, we've got doctors here. I don't want to sit around and smoke, we can drive out somewhere, Scarborough, Moonstone."

"I'm back on at six a.m." Now, it seems, Poulos was serious about medicine.

"Somewhere around here, Nahant, Revere, where was it she went out to commit suicide in *The Bell-Jar?* Sylvia Plath, she came from Wellesley. Let's go out there."

"Where do you think you are? You can't go swimming around here without a bathing suit." Now suddenly Marilyn was Ms. Reasonable.

"We can pick up suits, we can drive back to Wellesley, head out Route 128, let's do it."

Yvonne. Stretched out on the beach. She lies there, strands of seaweed in her hair. Her legs spread open, the tide is coming in, up, between her legs, it has almost reached the channel, it is pushing hard, it is throbbing. Open and close. In each hand a small smooth stone, clenched again and again, the beating of the sea.

I have heard these waves. This is what they say: All your fat will melt away! The pleasure center is not where you think it is. The mind is not only in the head; the eye is not only in the face. Beauty is more than skin deep; it is deeper; it is the only thing. The mouth says words you don't know the meaning of; the heartbeat changes with the seasons; the heartbeat changes with the waning of the moon.

This is the name of the color of the sea, the Rhode Island sea: once gray, once green.

Perhaps the color of smoke.

The moon is looking down.

There is no one in sight.

"We'll never make it to Wellesley and out to Nahant, back to Wellesley. We'd be driving all night." Vroom, vroom. Poulos took another deep drag. "Besides, I don't like to drive too much when I smoke."

Yvonne's legs, spread open on the sand, look like this: V.

That's what the goddess sees, Victoria in the heavens, and what her sister, the guardian, exquisite Pulchritudo, sees also.

"I don't care, it doesn't matter to me, but I don't want to stay here, the smoke hurts my eyes, it smells bad. Let's go outdoors, we can go for a walk in the Fenway, it will be pretty."

"You'll get mugged," Marilyn said happily. "You'll get raped by a black man."

"I'll take you out." Gallant Poulos. "We'll go for a ride and I'll take you home."

And touch?

No touching.

No more parties.

No more parties until the pageant parties at Atlantic City.

No more parties until the reception for the National Press. Until the TV Warm-up Party. Until the States

109

Mixer. Until the Atlantic City Chamber of Commerce Dance. Until the Miss New Jersey Welcome America Reception.

No more parties until the Farewell Party, with the queen standing in front of the carved wooden hotel throne and kissing each of the losers. Forty-nine of them. Excitedly, kissing every one of them Goodbye.

VIII

At the glittering court, all the Wellesley girls with their sashes, all the contestants in their gowns, waving their free-flowing hair back and forth, calling out, Hosanna, Save us, Io, Io, sometimes in Latin, sometimes in Greek, in all the languages ancient and modern. All the jewels of adornment are there, all the colors of the dove's neck, the anthology of the rainbow.

But Pulchritudo, Victoria, they are not there; they are above, members of another court, along with Aphrodite, sweet but terrible Ishtar, Iuno, all of them praising, singing their empyrean songs, the hymns raised by the Babylonians, Sumerians, Indians, Grecians, Latins, Etruscans, Mexicans; they rush about like the winds, they rise up and down like the breath of a woman in heat, the light is pink, red, iridescent, the color of the inside, almost blood at its deepest. They swirl about the hidden throne where she lies naked, the Great Queen, Her, Miss Rhode Island.

Ah, Julie, you have been found out. Marilyn, you have revealed yourself. Wave your arms! No! More gracefully than that, you are her servants. All praise, all praises to.

Fino had the balls to call again.

The answer: No.

Poulos called too. They're all coming round now, the fellows, they're getting hotter as the contest gets closer. "Come with me, why don't you?" Poulos said. "I'll take you swimming. I know a place. I know that place you wanted to go to. It looks out over to Nahant. I go out there sometimes. Let's go on Saturday."

"I'm sorry, thank you for asking, but I really can't. Listen, let me talk to you straight. I'm involved with someone else." His hands are the ones that move along Miss Rhode Island's thighs, it's his shoulders that get bitten at.

"Why were you at that party?"

"I was dragged along."

"Come on, I'll drag you along too. I'll take you to a movie, we used to have such a good time together." Over the phone his breath could be heard: Poulos had finally called.

"I can't. Next year. Call me after the pageant, wait until I'm Miss America. Wouldn't you rather go out with Miss America than just Miss Rhode Island? I'm in a funny position, I can't go out now."

"I don't care if you're Miss Nothing." This she could remember, Poulos wasn't one to take no for an answer easily. "Remember, I was after you before it happened. I knew you when."

"I can't, Arthur, I can't. I just can't. It's hard to make anyone understand. Don't take it personally. It isn't that I don't like you. Just bear with me if you can do that, I'm under so much pressure."

Poulos hung up.

But Fino called again. This time he called three days in a row. Finally Yvonne talked to him.

"I don't want to see you. No way. You can forget it. You never knew me."

"I just want to apologize. You never let me apologize." He waited a moment for her to say "That's all right"; she didn't say it. "Isn't there something I can do to make it up to you. How's your arm? It's O.K., isn't it?"

"Look, forget it. It doesn't matter anymore, it doesn't hurt anymore. I'm all cured." Her arm: soft, flexible, holding the receiver.

"They keep on bothering me," she said to Julie. "They don't let go."

"You love it!" One of Julie's standard lines. And the next day when she brought up the mail, she threw two letters onto Yvonne's bed, one from Poulos and the other from Fino.

"Rip them up," Yvonne said. "Do me the favor. If Truston knew about Poulos he would get mad."

"Do your own dirty work."

That night when Yvonne took off her bedspread, they fell onto the floor. "I don't want to touch them, throw them out for me."

"Why don't you throw them out yourself?"

They stayed there, but when Julie was out of the room Yvonne made sure she stepped on Fino's letter. Poulos's letter she carefully walked around. "Just do me the favor, why won't you do it?" she said the next day. "Throw them out for me."

So viciously Julie tore them up and threw them into the wastebasket.

"I don't think you've ever had a serious love affair," Yvonne said to Julie the next night. It was a Saturday; Julie's medical student, Gold, had stopped calling. Poulos had called again, though. Turned down.

Yvonne had taken a shower, Julie had taken a shower,

they were both in their room, Julie was putting on nail polish. It took a long time to do it right. "I am the Botticelli of the toenail," Julie said, "the Leonardo da Vinci, the way I paint this."

Marilyn, on the other hand, was going to bring somebody back to sleep over that night, that's what she promised.

"I don't think you can have a serious love affair with a college boy, with somebody who isn't really grown up yet."

"You can have serious sex."

"You sound like Marilyn."

"That's all a serious love affair is."

"Do you think that's true," Yvonne asked Truston, "a serious love affair is nothing but sex? Dante and Beatrice? Priscilla and John? Nothing but that?"

"Ninety-nine percent," Truston said.

But the dress Yvonne chose for the private interview with the judges covered all scars.

"This is the most difficult costuming decision," Mrs. Melli said before they bought it. They had looked in Filene's, they had looked in Bonwit Teller. "It has to be sexy, it has to be sexier than the evening gown, because that's sexy anyway; it has to be sexier than the swimsuit. The swimsuit, you're sticking out all over, you don't need to worry. But this dress, it has to look like a regular dress, you know what I mean. You wear it to a business interview, right? But it's got to do something really special for you, that's where they're going to get their best look at you. Forget about Talent, forget about Swimsuit, this is the real thing. They're going to ask you what's your favorite activity, you can't say the truth"—since she had learned about Truston, Mrs. Melli was full of innu-

114

endo—"they're going to ask you what's your favorite period of history, who's the favorite member of your family; and all the time they're going to be looking at your bust line."

"I know a nice store in Cambridge."

"Jordan Marsh in Framingham, that's nice. Better than Jordan's at the Warwick Mall. You might not think so, but it is."

They took the trip out to Framingham. But there was nothing decent there. As a result, they had to go to Cambridge. Walking through Harvard Square, Mrs. Melli looked out of place. "I hate this place," she said. "I think they're a bunch of damn snobs, my son went to Providence College, good enough. You know they don't say much about this anymore these days, but they're still Communists here, they always were. You didn't go out with any of these boys, right?"

"I did for a while. That's the one who broke my arm."

"Get rid of him. You did already. Your current has to be better than that one, no matter what, even if he's an old man taking advantage. If you said your boyfriend went to Harvard when the judges asked you, you might as well pack up right then and leave Atlantic City, kiss it all goodbye, forget it."

"My brother goes to Brown."

"That's all right, brothers, they don't count so much. West Point would be better, Annapolis. He ever try for an appointment? My son tried for an appointment, he didn't get it."

"There's a boy in my town who got appointed, but Joseph didn't try out. He always wanted to go to Brown from the first day he saw it; there it was, it looks so established. He likes it there. But I never wanted to go,

115

I wanted to be farther from home, not too far from Rhode Island, though. I'll be back, I said it at the contest."

"Pageant, dear." Evidently Mrs. Melli didn't much care what Yvonne talked about as they walked along. It was enough for her to chatter, practice on personality, outgoing qualities, charm.

"Pageant, right, it's the pageant, not contest. I shouldn't forget it. You know, I want to tell them this, I'm taking an art course—Rubens, Renoir, Titian, and I haven't seen one landscape as pretty as Rhode Island."

"You tell that one to the judges." Mrs. Melli sounded pleased.

The dress shop in Harvard Square pleased her too. "They got nice stuff, see this one?" She held up a pale blue-gray dress, it felt sheer but it wasn't; it was winter-bay-colored, a Rhode Island color if ever there was one. Anne Hutchinson could have worn that color; also the Vanderbilt heiresses at Newport the day their dukes proposed. It wasn't outstanding at first glance, but it stayed with you. Was it blue, was it green-gray? "Try this one on. This one is you."

"I think you can pull it in a little bit under the bust line," Mrs. Melli said when Yvonne came out of the dressing room.

"I hate to fool with it."

"I'll do it. Don't worry, as soon as you come back for vacation, come down to my house and I'll pull it in." Her hands tucked the dress in a little more under Yvonne's breasts.

Yvonne's breasts. Not so big as those of Alabama, Alaska, Arkansas, North Carolina, North Dakota, Ohio. Mrs. Melli had shown her a list of contestants. They all had statistics.

Yvonne was 36, a B cup going on C, almost C. But there were plenty of C cups in the pageant. There were every year, even some D cups, and not just California, not just the Carolinas, the Dakotas. One point of solace, two you might say if your mind ran that way, Yvonne had seen Connecticut. She was no great shakes, nothing spectacular.

"Rhode Island is not one of the most beautiful states." Truston himself admitted it to her. "Wait till you see California, Colorado. You've seen Vermont and Maine, you know them. But don't let that get to you, it doesn't have anything to do with the state itself. Look at Miss Mississippi, she's always winning. Alabama, there's nothing there but cotton fields, you can forget about that, it isn't the state. Get that out of your mind."

"Though Rhode Island is the smallest state in the Union, she is larger than ancient Attica." A quote from the *Rhode Island Fact Book,* one of her prizes. Providence was bigger than ancient Athens. It was built on hills like Rome. Yvonne knew: it was the state itself that counted.

That's why she wanted to spend time with Truston again at Moonstone Beach. "We don't have to go to bed there, we can just walk on the beach. You must think I'm superstitious, it's crazy, but we spend all our time out of state in Massachusetts. Rhode Island's so pretty. I'd like to be by the water. I'm never near the water here."

"Don't worry, I'll take you down there again sometime."

"How about now?" The car was heading down Route 9 toward Boston, on the way to the motel. "It'll have to be soon, the summer's coming."

"Next week. Is that soon enough?"

"Next week, I have to tell you. I can't see you."

A first.

117

The car swerved a little. "Who is he?"

"My God, look where you're going, we could have an accident."

"I'm a careful driver. Who is he?"

"It isn't anybody."

It wasn't Poulos.

"I have to go to a meeting."

"Is it that important? I can only get away on Tuesday next week."

On either side of them, there were neon lights: restaurants, discount stores, motels. "It's a meeting. I've been skipping it all spring and Julie's the president of the club. I'm involved, I should go."

"What kind of club?"

"Ecology. Greengirls it's called, and I have to go." They were turning into the blacktop driveway of the motel. "Because my brother is involved. Brown invited us to a joint cleanup, and I have to be there."

"Jesus!" The car stopped in front of the motel office. "A garbage pickup. Miss Rhode Island would rather pick up garbage than get laid." He shut his eyes. Neon, fiery red, was glaring on his face. "I'm sorry. That wasn't a nice thing to say."

"I can't help it, I feel responsible, my brother and my own roommate. The meeting's every other Tuesday and I haven't gone to one since March, that's why Julie's been so mad at me all the time." Truston had opened the car door. "There's going to be a vote on it, they need my vote, I have a responsibility. To society, too."

Could Miss Rhode Island neglect society?

"I'll be back in a minute." Truston got out of the car.

"Why don't you ever write me a letter?" Yvonne asked when he got back into the car and started driving toward his parking space. "You went to New York on business,

118

why didn't you send me a postcard? You don't even have to sign it, I won't blackmail you. I'll know who it's from."

"To my little pussy. Something like that? Is that what you want?" Truston stopped the car. Room number 3.

"You have a dirty mind. Just a letter. Hello from Rockefeller Center. I've never even seen Rockefeller Center. The only time we're ever in touch is when we go to bed."

Truston put his hand on her thigh lightly. He looked at her. He touched her chin and moved her face around to meet his look. His look, it meant this: Do you think that's bad?

To that there was no answer.

But wouldn't you think a lover would be able to send a letter from time to time? Even Fino managed it. Poulos did it. Even Joseph came across: "Dear Miss Rhode Island, All the members of the Brown Ecology Club are fans of yours. We're going to have a cleanup somewhere. Why don't you get some of your girlfriends together with us and we can have a joint Brown-Wellesley ecology project. Something like cleaning up along some highway, maybe off Route 95 somewhere."

"That's a nice idea, thanks for your letter." Yvonne had sent a postcard back. "My roommate Julie will send you the answer. She's the ecology chairwoman this year."

Tuesday evening, the choice: Truston or the Green-girls.

"Naturally I'm going to choose Truston," Yvonne told Julie. "I'm going to have to skip this meeting too. I told Truston I couldn't meet him, but then I changed my mind."

"It's only this one meeting. It's your own brother asking."

"I'd rather be with Truston."

119

This is the lover of nature, this is the contestant who planned to tell the judges at Atlantic City: "I'd do anything to improve the quality of the environment. Ecology. Nature. That's one of the things I'm interested in."

A letter from heaven, from the goddess: Stay with Truston! I am sending you messages all of the time. Delivered in that soft place. I get your letter, I feel it coming at me, T with its resolute thrusting. Wonderful T! Astonishing Y! These are the important ones, these are the letters that come.

"Do you think this is all right for an answer from the Greengirls?"

Yvonne took Julie's scented stationery into her white hands. Dear Joseph, Yvonne passed on to me your letter about the joint Brown-Wellesley cleanup in my capacity as chairwoman of the Greengirls . . . "Do you think this is all right for a beginning?"

"It seems fine. Why do you need my O.K.?"

"His letter was to you."

"It only went through my hands." Yvonne's fingers had brushed over it smoothly, Julie had held it between her palms. Now Joseph would rip open Julie's envelope, he would pull out the paper.

"Arrange it for a time when I can be there." Miss Rhode Island's look, her presence alone, removes dirt; the rusty cans, the soggy cardboard, the tinfoil, they are swept up as she passes by. "How about some Saturday morning? Anything but a Tuesday. But you'd better make it soon before exams start."

The project: an overgrown lot behind Main Street in Woonsocket. The Brown Ecology Club had decided to adopt Woonsocket.

The time: the second Saturday in May.

"I'd rather work on a beach," Yvonne said to Julie when the answer came from Joseph. "With a beach you can see exactly how much you have to do and you can clock your own progress."

"I like the idea of working with men." Julie was alongside her, climbing the Pomeroy stairs up to their room. "I'm sorry I didn't go to a coed school."

"Bring a pair of work gloves. You know, the kind they use for gardening. That's what I'm going to do. Otherwise your hands get messy."

"Why are you always worrying about things like that? It's ridiculous, like being in a beauty contest twenty-four hours a day."

"Now you don't have to be like that!" Politely Yvonne held the door of their room open so Julie could enter first. "It's just common sense, you could get cuts, you could get tetanus. We did a cleanup in high school once, one of the boys got a cut from a tin can, it was all rusty."

"Wear work gloves. You can buy them at the five-and-ten." Julie neatly lettered the words on the announcements she made to post in Pomeroy Hall and all the other dormitories on the Wellesley campus.

But it was overcast the morning of the second Saturday in May. Besides Julie and Yvonne, only four other girls showed up to be driven to Woonsocket in the cars that came up from Brown. Three cars, six girls. That worked out to only two girls each. Yvonne and Julie went in Joseph's Dart, Julie in the middle seat, right next to the driver.

It was less than an hour's ride. But one hour was enough for Joseph. When he and Julie got out of the car in the Woonsocket municipal parking lot, he had his hand on her back. "I should have told Mrs. Melli about

121

this," Yvonne said quietly when they got to the work site. "She would have had a photographer here from the Providence *Journal.*"

"You wouldn't ever have your picture taken in those things, would you?" Julie pointed to Yvonne's hiking boots; they were waterproof, but they weren't pretty. "And with those gloves?"

"Why not? For ecology." Yvonne bent over right away and picked up part of a broken bottle. Where to put it? Fortunately, one of the Brown boys had had the foresight to bring some trash buckets along.

Fortunately too, another one of the Brown boys had brought along a camera. He took one entire roll, only of Yvonne. Not a twenty-shot roll either, a thirty-six. "I thought I'd shoot something just for the Brown paper," he said, "but because you're Miss Rhode Island, maybe I can sell one to the Providence *Journal.*"

"Hey, wait a minute," Joseph called to him. "Wait up. Get one of those with me in there."

He stood posing with one arm around Yvonne and the other arm around Julie. As soon as the picture was taken he leaned over and gave Julie a kiss. Then he leaned over to the other side and kissed Yvonne too.

Is that an appropriate thing for a brother to do?

"Pig! Isn't one girl enough for you? You're the cock of the walk here," Yvonne said. "Mr. Clean!"

"Leave him alone. He did a good job. It was a good idea for us to get together." Was Julie speaking only in her capacity as chairwoman of the Greengirls?

On Yvonne's pink shoulders the heavy weight of Joseph's arm rested.

"She's a nice girl, your roommate."

"Ain't I?"

But Joseph was younger than Julie, younger than

122

Yvonne. Not that much younger, though, only two years.

Yvonne and Joseph! They had made an adorable pair as babies, with him looking up admiringly at her and her with an arm protectively around his shoulder. Now his arm was around hers.

Helen of Troy had twin brothers, Castor and Pollux. Yvonne had only one brother.

That made him all the more precious.

"Did you like my brother?"

Back at Wellesley, Miss Rhode Island walked through the quadrangle as smoothly as if she were on her skates.

"Slow down." Julie, the attendant, walking beside her.

"You've got to keep in shape. You walk too slow."

"I'm not in a contest."

"Never mind the pageant, for God's sakes."

"I thought he was very nice."

Very nice. That's not New England understatement, anybody would know that. That's something else, the voice of Ms. Fearful, the voice of I Want.

"I'll ask him if he's going to see you again."

"Don't do that."

"I'd like to, I'd like to have you hit it off. Wouldn't that be nice? It'd be a nice change. He had a girlfriend, I didn't like her."

"We could double-date with you and Truston. He's much younger than I am."

"All right, drop it, I won't say anything." They entered the door to Pomeroy Hall. "If you don't want me to."

"Now I'd really like to meet Truston, I changed my mind, I really mean it."

"You already met my brother, one ought to be enough for you."

A loser's statement. Is Miss Rhode Island flipping her cork?

But then when Joseph came up to Wellesley to visit Julie, it was "No, why should I mind?"

Of course, if it should happen to work out that way, Julie could have a friend stay over in the room, even Joseph. That was something Yvonne could not do. Could Truston stay over? Could Miss America have an overnight visitor in a Wellesley dorm?

"But why are you thinking like this now? You only met Joseph once, he's not that great, you haven't had anyone stay over yet this year. I'll sleep in Marilyn's room if you want me to, she's out practically every Saturday night anyway."

"Will you get your beauty sleep? Will it be all right for you sleeping on a strange bed like that, without your own pillow? Is it all right?"

"Knock it off, Julie. I don't mind. Remember, I was the one who wanted you to hit it off with Joseph."

"I feel funny pushing you out like this. What if he doesn't want to stay over, if it doesn't work out that he stays over and you spent the whole night wasting the time, sleeping out?"

"It'll work out, just don't worry about it."

"Maybe I should just have him come up during the evening just to visit like with both of us and then you can move somewhere else, find some excuse and go out and then we can have the room." Did Julie want Truston too? Could she be Miss America? "If it works out that way, that is."

The reason Yvonne had roomed with Julie originally was that Julie wasn't one of those girls who wanted to listen to music all the time. Julie didn't even have a stereo, she didn't have a guitar. That was a plus.

"Just make sure you don't tell him about Truston."

Yvonne could go stay with Truston in Providence overnight. She could go to New York with him for a weekend. They could walk down the street holding hands, he would take her to a movie, they would be ordinary.

"Do you think we're going to talk about you and Truston? Is that all we have to talk about?"

"Well, I hope you don't."

Appalling Julie answered, "I'll be too busy to think of it."

Too busy. Yvonne was certain of it. Joseph's stiff arms, his legs, his hips whipping up and down. So loud their creaking bed would be heard all over the dormitory.

Their bed? Her bed perhaps, not Julie's. Her scene. The music of the spheres. Wherever Yvonne has moved, the atoms spin.

Why?

Y. Perhaps that is the name of the still undiscovered indivisible particle of matter.

Late in the night, Yvonne unsleeping in the quadrangle outside Pomeroy Hall. In her room, lights out. But were Julie and Joseph asleep? Or were the atoms spinning, the particles joining with each other as Lucretius said when he wrote that "no rest is given the atoms in their course through the depths of space"?

"I really don't care what you do with Joseph. I don't care who you sleep with. Whom. That's nice." Yvonne said it the day after Joseph's visit.

"She knew I wasn't telling the truth, I don't want him sleeping with Julie, I don't want him around my friends, let him stick to his own." She was actually crying in front of Truston. It was only the second time, though. It would show on her face the next day, around her eyes. Miss

125

New York was dancing at a party given in her honor in Utica. Miss Tennessee was weighing herself cautiously; she had not gained a pound.

"Forget about him. Think about whom I'm sleeping with," Truston said.

Would one of Joseph's daughters become Miss America in time? One of the Arnolds? Arnolds were spread all over America, they had gone to Ohio, to Oregon, intermarrying everywhere; so had the Pratts, her grandmother's family, so had the Carpenters. Which of her great-grandmothers was flying through the heavens interceding with the goddesses to favor the other, the wrong descendant?

"I know of a family where the brother and sister really did it. Nothing happened, but they don't talk to each other now."

"That's horrible." It was enough to make Yvonne stop crying. "Let him do it with Julie, let him get Marilyn too."

Joseph rampant.

"Don't you think it's a little strange, you balling with my brother? Don't you think that's more than a coincidence?" Yvonne said to Julie when she was packing to go home to Rhode Island for a weekend. To touch base. For more than two weeks, Poulos hadn't called to try to ask her out again.

"You're reading too much into it. I don't care that much about him. You know sometimes I'm impulsive that way. On the first date."

"I better not let Truston near you."

"I don't want somebody old."

No Miss Rhode Island could say: "You don't know what you're missing." Truston that week had been ferociously active. It was good that she would soon be putting away for the summer the book that said: He is changed to a god, he who looks on her. Now she understood it.

"Will you come to Atlantic City on Labor Day weekend?" she said to Truston.

"You know what the answer is to that."

"I thought I'd ask anyway."

"Think of it this way. I won't be there, but you know I'll be thinking about you all the time. I'll see you on TV."

"Will your wife let you watch?"

"She does every other year."

"You mean you've been watching that all the time?"

"We watch it together."

"That's dirty."

"Don't you watch it?"

"I watched it maybe once, twice, when I was a kid in high school. That's the sort of thing you look at when you're in high school."

"All the Catholic priests, they watch it too. All the Negroes."

Then he was one of the watchers.

In Alabama, Miss Alabama, in Minnesota, Miss Minnesota walked with their lovers under the leaves of the overhanging trees. There are so many men in America. So few really beautiful women. Poulos, Fino, Kirby. Joseph, Truston. Plus strangers.

"Have you gained weight?" That's what Truston said when he picked her up the next week at Wellesley.

Why? Isn't a beauty queen ever supposed to eat a Hershey bar? Reese's Peanut Butter Cups, buy one of them, you get two in the package; buy two, you get four. Also, those little mints. While you're studying you can eat fifty of them without thinking. Poulos wouldn't mind.

Greeks liked girls with something to hold on to. Not that she would ever allow herself to get fat.

Oh, Truston, Mrs. Melli, you were right. Perhaps I really don't want to win. Even fat, I will be more beautiful than my mother. We should have sent in the black one, Miss Darkie. Instead we sent in a horse, Rhode Island always loses. Why? We have Newport, they really have it, the New Yorkers, we're visitors in our own town, they're taking over the university too in Kingston; the jigs are all over Providence; it was different when the Italians moved in, the Portuguese, even the ones from Cabo Verde; these are coming in from the South.

Someday when this is all over I am going to walk all along the Blackstone River, right on the bank all the way from Pawtucket up to the Massachusetts line past the mills. Maybe someday I can get a job in one of those mills.

The Arnolds never worked in the mills.

So what if the Doucettes did!

Where would we be without those mills?

Back with the Indians.

Now they have candy mills, turning out those little mints, a thousand a minute, that's how fast you can eat them.

The Trustons, the Clapps, they made their money out of mills.

He's only in his office in the daytime.

In the nighttime, I do my exercises.

Kneel on the floor. Feet close together. Lean your head back. Arch. The letter C. Touch your ankles. Not a fat girl's exercise.

May, June, July. On September 4, they do the choosing.

"Don't be so nervous, Truston,"

In the car, riding south. Late afternoon. "If I win then I win. What do you care so much for? I should be the one who cares."

"I care. I want to do it to Miss America."

"I think that's all you want out of it."

"That's plenty." He tooted the car horn. Twice. "But that isn't the only thing I like about you."

Was it a mistake to go to Moonstone? This was the last week before the house would begin attracting Truston's own wife, his children. "They like to come down Memorial Day."

"Maybe we shouldn't go there."

"They're not there yet."

"How do you know?" The car was in South County already, on Route 1. Past Wickford.

"I know." He took one hand off the steering wheel and held her hand, Miss Rhode Island's hand, surprisingly large. Was it too large? "My wife would say something, before I left the house. She wouldn't just go down here." Out of the window of the car, a beautiful view of Narragansett Bay, the West Passage. Beyond it Jamestown; beyond that the East Passage. In the distance, hazy, the island called Rhode Island.

"You don't know for sure, she could go without telling you. Maybe she's down there with her boyfriend."

"Not likely." Truston put his hand back on the steering wheel. "You can always see a car parked in front of the house from a distance. Right across the marsh grass."

"Maybe the car dropped her off and she's there anyway and the car went away."

"You're too suspicious."

"Well, I used to think you wanted me to win because you liked me. Now I know different. I'm worried she'll be in there. Let's go somewhere else, I'm scared she'll come in on us. Think what could happen, you want me to win." She put her hand on the steering wheel, dangerously, as if to move it away from his house. "If she came in on us, it could get in the papers. They'd take away the crown, Miss Rhode Island commits adultery."

"You're getting hysterical."

"Let's go to a motel."

"That's stupid. It's more risky. Anyone could see us then."

"Not up in Massachusetts. Let's turn around, let's go back up out of state."

"We can go park at the beach, at Moonstone, and then walk along."

"That's worse, you could bump into someone on the beach."

"Who's on the beach on a day like this?"

Right. It was cloudy, there was a high wind, it was getting dark, nobody would come to the beach at this hour. But in the nighttime some might come, they might lie there in the dark on the sand in the wind.

Was it that the sun was so low, almost sunset? The water was blood red. Every wave coming toward the shore looked plague-like, a surge, the great bloody flow.

"That's impossible," Truston said, "they only have red tide in the summer. I never saw it before in the spring."

But it had been a very warm day.

In the ocean, blood.

On the shore, stones. Smooth stones, big and little, polished by the waves and by the sand. Mostly quartz, milky quartz, white as ice, rose quartz, quartz with amethyst incorporated, smoky quartz with dead plants and animals hidden in the stone.

That's what Moonstone Beach is famous for. Once I was walking along that beach looking down among the stones—that way the stones are most beautiful, thousands of them, who can identify them, they all have different shapes and presences, but they all look alike—and I bent over and picked it up there, round and smooth and misty, so full that the depths of it were both visible and invisible; there it was, finally discovered: the authentic moonstone. I had picked up and discarded thousands of stones before I found it. But some of them I kept. I have them at home, lots of them, arranged in a line along the windowsill.

Another day I was walking along looking downward as always and suddenly I found it: the egg of the moon. Pure white except for this: tiny blood-colored threads could be seen here and there beyond the surface, the veins.

It is written that Aphrodite came out of the sea foam.

Before that time she was also beneath the waves in the egg of the moon.

The tide flows under the moon.

The moonstones, the eggs of the moon are tossed up onto the shore. They are pulled back into the sea under the moon.

"I can see nobody's in the house," Truston said, "but let's not even go in, let's stay right out here on the beach."

Above the sand and the stones, round and milky, stones like the breasts of the goddess Pulchritudo.

"Roll your leg over," Truston sang it. "Roll your leg over. Roll your leg over the man in the moon."

IX

This time it was Julie answering Yvonne's phone calls.

"He was that nice one with the Greek name."

"Onassis."

"No, not Onassis, the one who sent you the letter. I asked him if he wanted you to call him back. You know what he said? 'Never mind that, she won't do it, I'll call her again.' And then he called again not more than half an hour ago. I just got off bells. He sounds nice. No put-on. Even when he said you would never call back."

"Why don't you go out with him then? You shouldn't just stick with Joseph. He's fickle."

"I want you to go to a dance with me. The Copley Plaza." Poulos waited a moment for her answer. "My class is having a dance. The fifth of June. I know you're involved. It's a Saturday night, you probably can't get away."

"It's in the middle of exam period."

"It might do you good to get away. With me."

"I've got an exam in Latin poetry that Monday." Did exams stop nature? Did contests? "All right, Arthur, I'll go with you." Worrying about exams didn't stop Julie from going to the movies with Joseph and then, after the movies, rushing back to Wellesley; but it wasn't to study

Child Development. Julie already had the room reserved.

"We have trysts on weekends, not on Tuesday nights like you and your friend," Julie had said. "Do you mind going to Marilyn's?" A quick retraction: "You don't have to. Don't worry, I'm not really going to get involved with your brother, we won't get to be relatives. I'm too conscious of the age difference."

"Why are you going out with him then?"

"Ask Truston if you can't figure out the answer to that."

As if Yvonne were the whore just for being attracted to Truston.

"I'd like to meet this Joseph," Marilyn said when Yvonne asked her about the room. "He must be pretty good to get Miss Rhode Island out of her room and get in on Julie. Maybe I'll ask Julie if I can have a turn. But not this Saturday, I've got somebody coming myself."

"That's human nature," Julie said when Yvonne reported back. "This place gets like a massage parlor on Saturday nights. I think it gets worse in spring term. At least it's girls and boys. I have a friend at Sarah Lawrence, you know what goes on there."

"If I weren't Miss Rhode Island it wouldn't be a problem for me." Yvonne's icy profile, suitable for the judges.

"There you go, Miss Rhode Island again. Why should it make any difference?"

Because I am beautiful. Because I rode in on the foam. Because I have the golden spindle and the great golden jars. Because I have the two black beasts, large-toothed, one on either side. I have the infant. I have the black hole into which the great thunderbolt is cast; great as it is, in me it is encompassed.

"You can have the room. I'll find another place."

133

"You could bunk in with us."

"I'll go to Rhode Island for the weekend. I'll study down there. I have to talk to Mrs. Melli about Memorial Day. I have to get my dress ready. I have to polish up my crown, I bet it's tarnished already. I have lots of things to do."

"O.K. I'll go into the Providence Memorial Day Parade," Yvonne had told Mrs. Melli, "but only on one condition."

A smile. Mrs. Melli smiled when she was unhappy. "No conditions, dear."

"The condition is this: The float has to say, 'Miss Rhode Island supports ecology.' "

"No conditions." For Mrs. Melli negotiation was simply the repetition of her previous position.

If there were no conditions, the parade would be too tempting, the idol in procession while the worshippers bowed down.

"All right." Yvonne was defeated. "I'll go in your damn parade." She would have to wear her crown.

"Good, then we'll see what we can do to get an ecology angle on the float." Mrs. Melli's condition had been met, she smiled again. Happy or unhappy, keep smiling, a model.

Truston was away for the weekend anyway, down to Moonstone with his wife.

For the Doucettes, a dutiful daughter, faithful Yvonne. "I don't care if you don't come. Who wants to go all the way into Providence on Memorial Day in the morning? I wouldn't go if I didn't have to, it's silly. Better go down to the beach, stay out in the yard, it will be hot."

"Why don't you see, dear, if Emilie can ride with you on the float, it would be a thrill for her."

Is that the only reason her parents came? Because

Emilie, wearing her Rainbow Girl gown, rode next to her on the float throughout the parade?

Like the queen of England, Yvonne waved first to the right side and then to the left.

The ecology touch: On the float it said, "Miss Rhode Island. Keep Rhode Island Beautiful."

When a black dude, tall and well formed—he could be Mr. Rhode Island except for two things, one being that there was no Mr. Rhode Island; he was wearing green pants, almost silken, and a green armless shirt, he was looking up at her, his skin shining—called out, "Come on down, baby, I want to give it to you," Yvonne stuck out her tongue.

"That's disgusting. How can you stand it?" On the float at knee level, Emilie was distressed. The expression on her face, like the proportions of it, made it clear she would never be Miss Rhode Island.

"I get used to it, I don't let it bother me, they all act the same, he's just more outspoken." Yvonne smiled harder. "They're a bunch of idiots."

Emilie didn't smile. "I don't think he was nice."

"They're fools." Yvonne blew a kiss to an old man sitting in a wheelchair by the side of the road. "I wouldn't go two minutes out of my way to see Miss Anything." Suddenly she caught sight of Truston standing in the crowd.

"I don't think you should have stuck your tongue out at him."

"Shhhh!"

"Why? Nobody can hear us." They were seated at the back of the float.

"Shut up." Yvonne turned her head. Slowly she was being carried past Truston. She stared at him. In that crowd, he didn't seem taller, handsomer, more compelling than anybody else. He waved at her, he moved his mouth, he was saying something, silently. What it was she could not tell.

"I like riding in the parade." Emilie started waving at people too. "I don't think I could ever be Miss Rhode Island, though, I don't think I'd even be chosen."

"You could be chosen, cookie." Truston was back out of sight, there in the crowd. He had driven up from Moonstone just to see her for maybe a minute wearing her crown, just to see the people cheering her. "Maybe it will happen to you, nobody knows, you can't tell who it will happen to, that's part of the thrill of the whole thing." She began smiling again. Even when two teenagers, Italians, standing next to a lamppost caught her eye and called out, "Eat it, eat it, baby," she didn't stop smiling.

"She has to listen to this awful talk, I'd hate it, the things they say." Emilie was sitting in the back of the car as they were driving back to Wickford.

"I told you, I don't listen." Miss Rhode Island angry again, sitting stiffly in her gown, looking at her landscape going by. Her crown was on her lap. "I don't listen."

Listen, listen, they are coming at you, all the noises, out of the earth, they speak from the crevices, try to hurry by in the automobile, it is no good; the automobile itself will be heard: vroom, vroom.

"I don't listen to them, I don't give a damn, they have their dirty minds, I don't have that kind of dirty mind, so it's meaningless to me." As, question mark, it is meaningless to Truston my lover, walking on the beach to the sound of the tide, waiting for the new goddess to rise up out of the waves. Once a year.

"I told you, Yvonne." That is a mother's right, reminding a child of how correct she is. "I told you that

136

would happen, they'd all be after you." Charlotte twisted around in her seat, even her safety belt couldn't restrain her. Her two breasts turned toward her two daughters. "I told you it would be like that."

"She can handle herself." Yvonne's father had to keep his eyes on the road, he couldn't look at the three females, even in the rearview mirror. The portion of the father: to avert his eyes, to look straight ahead, driving toward the destination without imagining the bodies as they are, only as they might be, mangled, gaping, if he swerves to look at them, the long relaxed satisfying stare.

Turn, turn. Onto the exit for Wickford, Scenic Route 1A.

That great clock, earth, is turning too. We are having Memorial Day. We will have the Fourth of July. Then Labor Day, the pageant.

"Why did you come, Truston? To the parade, I mean. It made me feel funny."

"Well, I won't be able to go to Atlantic City. I wanted to see you in your natural habitat. I wanted to see you perform."

"I wasn't doing anything. I was just sitting there waving."

"That was all I wanted to see."

"I love to look at you," Poulos said. They were dancing, an old-fashioned dance. The medical school had mostly slow dancers. She was wearing a flowered dress with spaghetti straps. "I shouldn't say it, you'll get a swelled head, but you always turned me on. I'm not talking marriage, I don't want to be rash, but I'd like to come home to you every night. That would be something."

"You just think about sex all the time."

"I'm a doctor, it's O.K. I've got some perspective on

137

the whole thing. But I don't think about sex all the time, it's just that when I get near you that's what I think of, not even sex. Just touching you, you're so beautiful."

Poulos said it.

Truston said it.

"I can't believe anybody else in that contest is going to be as pretty as you are." She was lying in bed with Truston in the motel room on the Worcester Turnpike. "Look at your nose." How could she do that unless she had a mirror? He ran his tongue over it, he kissed it. "It's perfect. It's a perfect nose. Look at your neck."

"Don't make a mark on it."

"Did I ever do that?"

Never on the visible places.

They had already finished. Soon they would go out to dinner at an Italian restaurant nearby. He wanted a whole meal.

"I don't like to think that way, lots of girls are just as pretty. I wish you could meet my friends, maybe you're right about that. You should meet them, they're pretty. I wish we could go out sometime on a double date, just get together for coffee the way everyone else does, but I know that's not possible."

He had his hand on her. She felt the heavy stroking.

"Sometimes Marilyn feels this, she imagines all the other women in the world have disappeared, they're all gone, and she has her choice of every man. They all want her and she lives in a penthouse in New York on Fifth Avenue. I practically haven't ever been to New York, you were going to take me to New York one time, remember? And she has bodyguards who do everything she says and who protect her and a different man comes in every day, she looks at the pictures and chooses them and some-

138

times two a day or three, if she feels like it. And then, do you know what happens?"

"She sounds like she's the one who ought to be Miss America."

"And then do you know what happens?" His hand felt like granite on her soft body, too heavy. He got on top of her. "Stop it, I was telling you something. Come on, Truston!"

But he pushed, he felt like the Washington Monument pushing her, Bunker Hill, his hands immense peninsulas, his shoulders Adirondacks.

"That hurts, Truston. Take it easy."

"I know what happens. I can imagine it, three or four a day."

"That's not it."

Should she cry? Wouldn't he?

"This is what happens."

It didn't hurt so much now. Maybe she had turned to granite too.

A shout.

"She has a baby!" In the next motel room, they could hear it, they could hear it over the traffic on the road outside. "A baby!"

Truston didn't slow down.

"Whose baby is it? Mine?"

Yvonne tried to roll away. Unsuccessful. She would never win.

"Everybody's baby," she said. Stone. But it wasn't stone she turned to. Stone doesn't cry, tears don't come out of it, even when you hit it very hard, the way wood cries, tears actually come out of it, water drops, if you hit it hard with a big heavy hammer again and again and again.

139

"We'd love to have her come for the entire six weeks," the camp director said. Mrs. Coyle was her name. "We'd be honored, the girls would be thrilled to have a Miss America with them, it would give them inspiration."

Yvonne's toes curled down inside her shoes. Not a skater's reflex. "Miss Rhode Island, not Miss America."

"It would do your girls a world of good." Mrs. Melli, right in there against negativism. "It would be good to get you out of town."

"Of course, she would have to pay full fee. We have our rink, the counselors, we have to support them. And since she can't teach herself, but you're there to learn, dear."

$180 on the gown. $54 on the shoes. $70 on the bathing suit. And now another $1000 or $1200 for figure-skating lessons.

But patch time at the rink in Cranston would cost $500 over the summer. Plus driving up every day. Plus the lack of privacy, rehearsing in Rhode Island. The camp had its own rink, she could work at night, she could practice, she could control the sound system herself with nobody from Rhode Island looking on, not Mrs. Melli, not the reporters from the Providence newspaper—"Miss Rhode Island practices at Cranston Rink." None of that, only a bunch of little girls, figure-skating freaks, who would spend their summer looking up to her, little sisters, after Wellesley, a reward.

"We can send Emilie there too. I bet she'd love to go." It was Yvonne's own house, but in it her mother seemed like a guest of Mrs. Melli.

"No way. I don't want any distractions."

"Emilie won't be a distraction." The mother of Miss Rhode Island was also the mother of an ordinary Rhode

Island girl; indeed, she had, before the coronation, been an ordinary Rhode Island woman herself.

"Anything would be a distraction."

Lyndonville, Vermont. On somebody else's land. But Miss Vermont was no threat. And it was practically in Canada. It was true, on the radio in Lyndonville, you could hear French programs regularly.

"It will do you good to get away from the pressure." Even Mrs. Melli recognized it.

It was a deal. Six weeks, $1200, plus a new pair of skates.

"But I don't know what music to practice to." To Mrs. Coyle she admitted it. Mrs. Coyle was peppy and curly-haired. Off the ice too she wore a very short skirt.

"How many minutes are you working to?"

"Three."

"Two and fifty seconds." Always Mrs. Melli had the exact information.

"How would you classify your skills. I ought to see you skate."

"Not very advanced."

Mrs. Melli was right in there. "She looks beautiful. You look lovely on the ice, graceful. I've seen the Ice Capades, she has the capacity, I think so." She winked at Mrs. Coyle. "She's much too modest. They always are, all of them. If you asked her her measurements, she'd probably underestimate too."

"I'll see you skate. I'll pick out some music for you. Don't worry, I'll work out a good routine." Mrs. Coyle laughed. "Call me Roberta, we'll be down in Atlantic City to root for you. I always wanted to go to Miss America. This is the perfect chance."

"I'll introduce you around as Miss Rhode Island's skating coach. It will be worth your while, I think." Mrs.

141

Melli pulled a little notebook out of her pocketbook and wrote something down. "But I have to check it out with them down there first."

"Are there any other figure skaters in the pageant?"

"Wyoming."

"My God, I didn't know. How do you know?" Yvonne had never thought to ask.

"They sent us a list."

"We ought to make sure they don't use the same music. How can you check that out?" Coyle and Melli, co-conspirators.

"I'll make sure, I can find that out easy. Let's us pick what we want and decide fast, then we send that on to Atlantic City and then we've got that song sewed up, they can't use it—that is, unless they already sent theirs in. Could be they're waiting for us. They might want to psych Yvonne here out, figure out how good she is and then work accordingly. Push the strong points. One thing, you aren't supposed to let anybody see her work out. They might have some other people trying to see, you know what I mean."

"That's the advantage of a camp. You have complete control over who comes in."

"I don't want anybody watching me." In Vermont, Yvonne spinning unsteadily.

"Just the girls will watch her. The campers will love you, dear. They'll be so happy to have you."

"She'll get used to it. You've already been on TV once."

"You might be a natural, dear. I can have you doing layback spins in no time. They always love that. You watch the Olympics? They always do those. You let your hair grow a little longer, it helps."

"I can't. My hair stays the way it is, I have a good cut,

142

it's perfect for my face shape, you don't want to mess with too many things."

"She's right. No fooling around with the hairdo." Mrs. Melli spoke with authority, as if it were she, not Yvonne or Mrs. Doucette, paying the bills.

Oh, Truston, your true love is going away. To the north of Vermont.

Will it be Lake Memphremagog for you this year, Trus, no more Moonstone Beach? Do you have a yearning for the mountains, do you want to climb up? There's a green hill far away, there's lots to do up there, you could take in the music festival over at Caspian Lake, there are good trails for walking there. Did you ever canoe downriver under the mountains from Maidstone south? I did, it's so still there, the current carries you down, there's green on both sides of you, on the one side New Hampshire, on the other Vermont, and there you are going down right between them. The hills are so high, it doesn't take but a short time for the sun to go from up in New Hampshire to down in Vermont. Soon it's time to make camp up along the riverbank. It's easy to fall asleep after a day on the water, even solo. And if you do lie awake for a time in your sleeping bag looking up at the sky, it isn't Yvonne you start thinking of. It's time. It's how many days are remaining. How many nights are left? How much time before death comes? The end of the contest.

X

The future stands up ahead of you at the end of the runway, angry like a policeman, tall and blue. But not with the features of Truston, that is the past and still also the present.

"I'll never nag at you to get a divorce. I don't believe in that sort of thing. Here I'm leading my life, you're leading yours. Don't imagine I'm going to want to marry you, even if I don't become Miss America. I've got two more years of college, plus graduate school probably."

"I don't have to worry. I'm not the marrying kind."

"Why did you marry your wife?" When Yvonne was ten years old and had asked her father the same question, the answer had come out: "So we could have you." Now it was almost the same. "So I could get to meet you. God had it all planned."

"Did she?" Just because Yvonne was a beauty queen didn't mean she couldn't be a feminist too.

A frog. A snake. A squirrel. A clam. A box turtle. Of all the wild animals left in Rhode Island, none was impressive enough to be God. In Texas, the mountain lion. In Montana, the eagle. The wolf in Minnesota. Upon the beaches, dead skates. In the marshes, in the salt ponds, in Card Pond itself, the molted feathers of the ducks,

144

disintegrating. The gulls fly over looking for something to kill.

"Truston"—he would not be surprised—"I think I won't be able to see you all this summer."

"What do you mean?" He was surprised. "What are you talking about? It's easier, I don't have to come all the way up to Wellesley. We can meet somewhere in Providence. You have a car you can get your hands on, right?"

"I've got one for a year but I don't use it. I have to go to Vermont, I have to go to skating camp up in Vermont. But anyway it doesn't matter." She almost swallowed the words. "I ought to stop seeing you."

"Shut your eyes." He was driving her back to Wellesley. It was an afternoon, extra, a Thursday after a Tuesday, this week twice a week. He stopped the car. In front of a house. There were children in the front yard. A white house with green shutters. That house, remember it from the movies of your childhood, remember it from the insurance commercials, the beautiful street? The advertisement says: "One of these houses will be struck by tragedy this year. Will it be yours?" Death, it is coming, it is coming to someone on the street, is it coming to Truston? Who's going to get it? Maybe it will be me, I have lived on that street. It might be you. I hope it's you before me; it couldn't be Yvonne. Do beauty queens die, shouldn't they live forever, have they become immortal?

On the grass, the children, a boy and a girl were playing catch, the girl older, bossing. They looked up curiously: grown-ups had driven up to park in front of them. Truston moved the car ahead, halfway to the next house, stucco. Would it strike there?

"It makes no sense, but I feel I have to stop." She closed her eyes.

"Listen, forget it, stop worrying. Next week you'll be

home from school, you'll be in Rhode Island. I'll pick you up, you call me at the office. I'll pick you up some-where."

"They'll watch everything I do."

"I'll pick you up, I'll drive you somewhere, nobody ever goes there, we'll have the chance just to sit together in the car. Talk and take it easy."

Where would it be, off Route 3, the woods of Arcadia? Mount Hope where the cherry birches ripple in the wind? The Great Swamp where the Indians molder, where the war-fire in winter awakened the snakes and made them glide away into the waters of the great pond?

Glide away.

Frightened but moving slowly.

"Julie, do you know what I think?" Yvonne cautiously introduced the subject when she got back to Wellesley, even though she had a headache. "I think you'd better shop around to make arrangements for another room-mate for next year." She was retacking her map of the United States to the wall for one more week. The push-pin had fallen off one corner of it—sad to say, the north-east corner. "In case I win, just in case, you know there is a possibility, and then I won't be here for the year."

"I don't want to have to worry about that now." Julie was sitting at her desk trying to study. She still had two more exams. "It's hard to live with you, but I couldn't live without you."

"Maybe Marilyn won't want to be in a single room again."

"She needs it for her sex life. All those sleep-overs. One thing I like about you is no sleep-overs. You keep it under control." Julie looked up from her book to smile at Yvonne. "You do have a few positive things to recommend you as a roommate. It's not all bad. There's hope for you, Yvonne."

"What'll you do if I win?"

"I'll cross that bridge when I come to it. If I come to it. Actually you only have one chance in fifty. Two percent."

"I think I'd like to make a change." Yvonne had taken off her shoe. With the heel she began banging the pushpin into the corner of the map. "If I'm back here next year." The hammering was loud. "I think it would help the friendship."

"Who are you kidding? Say it right out, I don't give a damn." Julie shut her book, she got up, she went over to her dresser and began to rummage for something in a drawer. "You're right. Actually I think it would be a good idea. I didn't want to suggest it to you. I didn't want you to feel rejected right before going in for your contest there." She pulled a portable iron out of the drawer. "We'd both be better off."

"I'm glad you're not mad about it." Miss America, a diplomat. "I don't want it to be a sticky situation."

Julie plugged in the iron. "Don't worry about it. You have to keep your head nice and empty for the contest." She began to spit. But the iron didn't sizzle yet. By the third spit, the iron sizzled furiously. Julie put a towel on her desk and on top of that, out of the same dresser drawer, a scarf, the sling, Yvonne had given it to her. "Don't wear it around here," Yvonne had said. "I hate it, but it's a good scarf, and I shouldn't just throw it away." Fino's recompense to Yvonne, Yvonne's to Julie.

Julie went over to the sink and wet her hand so she could sprinkle water drops on the scarf. "I've been

147

meaning to iron this for a while." She held the iron's hot surface up, forward so Yvonne could see it.

Not close enough. It was not dangerous. Julie wasn't going to throw it. Julie couldn't do that, nobody could do that, they couldn't hate her that much. There wouldn't be a scar, a horrible red burn on her cheek. She wouldn't have to walk everywhere with a veil over the burned part of her face: Miss Hiroshima.

That was not what the goddesses had planned for her.

Julie put the iron down heavily on the scarf. Not enough water! When she lifted the iron there was a V-shaped scar, brown and crisp, over the center of the scarf.

V for vanquished. V for vanity.

"You burned it on purpose."

"That's crazy."

"You've been acting like a bitch ever since I won the contest. All you do is pick at me and make jokes."

Julie bent over to unplug the iron. She held it up. It was still hot.

"It's been no fun sitting here since you became Miss Hurrah there, watching you do those stupid exercises, acting like you were going to break if anyone looked at you cross-eyed." She rolled up the scarf and threw it into the wastebasket. Just where Fino's letters had gone. "All right, you're pretty, Yvonne, but you're not that pretty, I've seen prettier. There are prettier girls right here at Wellesley and don't think everyone doesn't know."

"It's not judged on pretty. It isn't a beauty contest." Yvonne's shoe was still in her hand. A weapon. Even without using it her headache was gone. She sat down on her bed and put it on.

"Bullshit. That's what they tell you. It's judged on who do you want to go to bed with, that's what it's judged on,

148

who's everyone after. And you love standing up there wiggling around. Don't deny it. That's why you got into it. I can see you at a party. That's the way you act. It's embarrassing. What do you think your friend Truston there is in love with? Not you, baby. But I want to tell you everybody knows just what it's all about. And you're the one who knows it best of all."

"Get out!" A scream. Could anyone hear it down the hall?

Julie turned to her like the winner of a pageant, triumphant, a quarter pivot at the edge of the runway. "I can't get out, I live here."

Is this Miss Beautiful, her mouth twisted? Miss Tranquillity? Her hands white as ice, but her face red. "Nobody would ever choose you for Miss Anything, you'd lose. I won't even tell you what my brother said about you." Because, discreetly, he had said nothing? "What would you pick at if I didn't win Miss Rhode Island? You don't even get decent marks."

It was true. Julie was going to flunk Child Development.

"I shouldn't get down to your level, but I want to tell you this, Julie." Yvonne went over to the closet door to get her pocketbook hanging on the doorknob. "I hate rooming with you. I hate your personality."

A victory: When she walked out of the room she didn't slam the door.

Downstairs in the entrance hallway Yvonne put a dime in the pay phone. It was 7 p.m. But she called Truston's office number anyway. Collect.

No answer there.

"If I press down on you, if I lie on top of you and press down hard and you shut your eyes," Yvonne said to

149

Truston, "and if you count to twenty-five and recite the magic word, it will be like the outline of my body is tattooed on you." Cool motel light. The air conditioner was off, so the bed and the room smelled harshly of other people's tobacco smoke. "Spread your fingers out so I can put my fingers on them. Put it inside me. Yes, like that. No, don't move. Keep still. Move your face so I can lean my cheek on yours. That's right. Am I heavy?"

"No."

"Don't move, I said." Above his chest, her soft breasts. Above his hips, her hips. "Now say this: V for victory."

"That's stupid."

"Say it."

"V for victory."

Above his thighs, her thighs.

"V." Above his belly, her belly.

"Now face the other way. Move your cheek and I'll press my other cheek out."

"What the hell's going on?"

"Almost finished. Say the words."

"Why? I already did."

"Go on, don't be bashful."

"V for victory."

"Now say Y."

"Why?"

"Now the lines are on your body."

"Can I move now?"

But instead, Yvonne moved.

"What are you doing that for? Don't let it slip out."

But it was too late.

"It was hurting me."

"I'll start different this time."

"No, that's enough for today." Yvonne got up. "Now you walk. Toward me."

150

"What the hell's going on?"

A fluorescent pink outlined on his body, like cheap-girl lipstick. She could almost see it. A mystery.

"I can't sleep with you anymore, Truston."

"What are you talking about?"

"I can't, I have to get ready for the pageant."

He reached his arms around her, one finger started to work, he picked her up. Their eyes were level.

"Put me down, Truston."

No play.

He let go of her.

"It's three months away. I said to myself I wouldn't sleep with anyone until the pageant, but then you came along and so I changed my mind. But now I have to hold off. Ninety days. Maybe after September."

"You're crazy. We're just getting started. You better hold on to me if you want to be a winner. You don't know how to win without me, you don't even want to win unless I'm around."

"You can go out and make the factory girls pregnant. All those Frenchies you talk about."

"Come on, Yvonne, you don't mean it." His shoulders looked pink. Maybe he had been out on Moonstone Beach with his wife.

"Three months." You had me once a week, sometimes twice a week, twice in one night. Look at me on TV.

Vee, vee. The voice of the Arnolds.

Along the roads, through the trees, through the marsh grass, on the surface of the salt ponds, in the old sawmills up in the woods. Only a woman out of America can be Miss America. Miss Idaho: "Nothing is so good and beautiful as this." That is what her great-grandfather had written back to upstate New York. You would feel it too if you saw that land, those rippling bare hills, that empty

151

air. Before Idaho, New York: before New York, Massachusetts. Miss Hawaii, she had some Hawaiian blood in her. Miss Texas was out of the pioneers who cut through the sweet woods along the trail westward. It wasn't only Miss Rhode Island who was an Americana of the Americanos. But her Arnolds had stayed planted in one place, hiding in the woods, lying low among the dune grasses. First there is faithful, then there is obedient, then truthful, then there is industrious; beautiful is not on the list.

She was small like Rhode Island: she had two broad legs like Rhode Island; she was spread open like Rhode Island; there was a great gulf up into her like Rhode Island. They could put her atop the capitol dome.

Could she then be America too, wide-breasted and fertile?

"There's no way to find out who the judges are," Mrs. Melli said over the phone. Yvonne had been home a week. Mrs. Melli had called twice. "You've got to bring your brother, Joseph," Mrs. Melli had said. "You've got to bring your little sister, not just Mom and Dad." To a barbecue at her house in Barrington. "They're celebrities too, but that shouldn't faze you, if you're going to be Miss America, you get used to celebrities."

She would be a celebrity at ice-skating camp in Vermont.

Vermont. Now she was nervous even coming to the other side of the bay to Barrington, even though it was still in Rhode Island.

When she had come back from Wellesley, sitting in the front seat next to her father, the back seat piled with books, on her lap a box holding ice skates, she felt a cloud clearing inside her head as soon as she passed the sign that said, "Entering Rhode Island." She was certain she looked prettier.

"A celebrity and a pretty one too," her father had said, at the Melli barbecue.

Mr. Melli was a large, broadly muscled man wearing a chef's apron. Melli, construction, bulldozers, shovels. Doucette, numbers, cuff links: he was an assistant to the comptroller at Swank, Inc., in Attleboro. They had almost nothing in common.

"If I was one of the judges," Melli said, "I'd pick Rhode Island as number one. But I'm not a celebrity."

"Hey, Yvonne!" Doucette's contribution. "Why don't you show us how you're going to walk up the aisle?"

"What's your favorite song, Yvonne?" Joseph the judge. As if it were a game. "Who's your favorite movie star?" Maybe Joseph would be a celebrity someday. He was as good as Kirby, as outspoken. An ordinary family, and now they're so famous. Her, Miss America; the brother, a celebrity; and the little sister—the little sister, nothing yet.

"Why don't you stand in for me," Yvonne said to Emilie, "because you're going to have to go through this someday too, I bet. What's your favorite song?"

"The Rhode Island Fight Song." Emilie had the right answer.

"Isn't she a darling. I'll be watching for you in a few years, Emilie." Mrs. Melli went over to her and gave her a hug. Emilie was wearing a sunsuit with straps that would have stayed up if she had a more developed bust line. With the hug, one shoulder strap slipped over her arm. "These things are loose, Ma," she said.

"Never mind," Mrs. Melli put her hands on Emilie's shoulders. "Show Yvonne how to walk down the runway."

153

"There she is, Miss America," Mrs. Melli sang in a deep voice, almost baritone. Or was that Mr. Melli joining her? It was loud, Joseph applauding, even Doucette sang along. "There she is, your ideal." A deep chorus, it was relentless. Only the dogs, locked in the cellar of the house, were ominously quiet; only her mother, standing next to Yvonne on the cement patio, was as quiet as the sky above them.

"This is nice," Yvonne said, "but it would be good to get some beach in today too. Why don't we drive down after lunch? I've never been to the town beach here. I brought my bathing suit."

Mr. Melli pressed his spatula heavily on a hamburger. It sizzled. "This one's for you, Yvonne. My wife, she don't like to go swimming."

"We just got here, Yvonne." Her mother's message: It might be all right for Miss Rhode Island to be impolite, for Miss America. But for Miss Doucette, it wasn't all right.

"Then we could come right back. After I have that hamburger over there, I don't want to miss that. Just to take a dip and then come back, it's hot." Yvonne moved away from the patio, away from the charcoal grill onto the grass.

"You go. You kids go. We'll sit here and drink." Mrs. Melli had set up her yard so you could sit anywhere in comfort and drink. Everywhere there were large coasters that looked like sunflowers on pointed sticks. If you got up and moved your lawn chair into the shade, you could move your drink holder too.

"Why don't you come along with us. I bet you look O.K. in a bathing suit too. It would be more fun if we all went together."

154

Joseph had the explanation. "You just want to show yourself off in a bathing suit, Yvonne."

"Leave her alone." Now the dogs could be heard growling from the basement. "They smell the hamburg." Mrs. Melli understood. "Yvonne needs to go swimming, she's going to be out of Rhode Island all summer up there in Vermont, it will do you some good, you ought to go down the beach."

"You come along."

"I'll stay here and do the dishes, I'll stay with the dogs, Jackie's pregnant anyway, I don't go to the beach no more."

"Why not?"

Should Yvonne have asked?

"You know, people get older, people go through changes, you can't do all the things you used to do, I had an operation." Mrs. Melli leaned over and whispered. "Mastectomy. I don't go down the beach no more. We used to have a place down Matunuck. I shouldn't have stayed out in the sun so much. That's how you get cancer, that's one of the ways." Now Mrs. Melli was talking loud. "Don't smoke, Yvonne, promise me you won't ever be a smoker, don't eat too much fatty foods, you got to take care of yourself. But you go to the beach."

"Maybe we shouldn't go," Yvonne said.

"Go! Go on, don't be silly." Another whisper. "A radical. All the way into the armpit. You could never tell. Could you ever tell? But at the beach you could tell."

"I could never tell."

Because it was unspeakable.

She would never tell.

She wouldn't even go to the beach.

155

"Come! Come with me!" The ancient harsh voice of Yvonne's grandmother. Grand'mère, she never spoke French, although her own mother had and her mother before her, and hers, back down to the time before French existed; and before then, they spoke the Latin language. A deep voice for a woman, even for a grandmother. "Come with me!"

But Yvonne had to do the driving. Superhighway all the way. "Use your official car, use it, don't be shy about it," Mrs. Melli had said. "Flaunt it." So Yvonne's grandmother edged herself, a shrunken woman, into the front seat of the Camaro with the license plate MISSRI. It looked like an advertisement for Miss Missouri, not Miss Rhode Island.

"I hate this car." Beneath Yvonne, the smooth vinyl seat, smooth as her skin. All spring the car had rested in a garage on Route 1 in Wickford; you couldn't take it up to Wellesley.

"Don't knock it, it's a beautiful car. Don't keep knocking what you got." Along both sides of Route 146 from Providence into Fall River, bright green. Inside the car, gray-white hair. Outside, trees budding nuts, fruit. Inside, gray-white eyes; thin lashes, almost gone; dry breathing. "What you got is swell."

As St. Anne, the grandmother spoke to her own progeny.

St. Anne's Shrine in Fall River had a big golden A set high above the door. A for excellent. A for first place.

"I know you're going to win the Miss America." But Yvonne had to take her grandmother's arm to help her up the steps into the church. Even though her grandmother also held on to one of the railings set along the staircase to aid invalids in climbing up to pray for a cure.

Only fifteen steps, but the way her grandmother struggled to climb them made Yvonne short of breath.

"I should have brought along the cast I used when I broke my arm, I should have put it up there." A stack of crutches was on display beside a marble statue of St. Anne. A red robe, a white gown. Behind her, an aureole of gold.

"Don't make jokes!" If Yvonne had been raised French, she would have been Catholic. But she was raised Episcopal. Miss Rhode Islands were always Catholic, Miss Americas always Protestant. Almost always. But had that been changed by the election of John F. Kennedy, of Jacqueline Bouvier of Newport? Of Yvonne Doucette of Wickford? Peut-être.

Her grandmother knelt down in front of the altar railing. She had to grasp the railing and lower herself slowly; it took her a long time to get down. When she was down, she tested herself, settling back on her heels once or twice—that shrunken bottom, once it had been round, now it was wrinkled—and she looked up, twisting around, and whispered loudly to Yvonne, "Kneel down!"

Dea Casta.

Genitrix.

Yvonne knelt too.

But it was early in the morning. There was nobody around to see.

"Oh, Holy Virgin, please answer my prayer.

"Guard Yvonne when she is competing in the contest, don't let her fall down again, don't let her hurt herself ice skating, don't let her trip. Holy St. Anne, make her Miss America. You say it too, Yvonne, come on."

"I feel funny about it."

157

"Come on, you're already kneeling down."

Over her shoulder Yvonne could see a nun in a short dress coming down the aisle of the church.

Quickly. "Holy St. Anne, make me Miss America."

"Say Blessed Virgin too."

"Blessed Virgin, make me Miss America." Yvonne covered her face with her hands, hiding her blue eyes, hiding her petal lips. Her soft knees hurt from kneeling. Could kneeling make a mark?

"Oh, Holy St. Anne!" A cracking, sexless voice. Her grandmother sounded like the priest on the radio. "Give this girl what she wants, let her be Miss America, let her win the talent contest, let her bring credit on her family, for the sake of the Blessed Virgin, Amen. Say Amen, Yvonne.

"Cross yourself."

"I'm not a Catholic." Yvonne, independent, stood up.

"Cross yourself."

"I feel funny."

"I'm going to stay kneeling here until you do."

That one worked.

"I'm sorry you took me there," Yvonne said on the ride back to Woonsocket.

"I still wish we hadn't gone," she said as she was climbing up the shining wooden stairs to the middle floor of the three-decker house in which her grandmother lived.

"I took Evangeline when she wanted to get into Bryant. She didn't have good marks but she got in anyway and now she's doing fine. That worked, this'll work. Don't you be worried."

Evangeline Doucette, Yvonne's cousin, lived on the bottom floor. She was a year older than Yvonne. She was studying law enforcement, her mother was Italian. Miss

158

Woonsocket, Miss Three-Decker; even for that one she wouldn't even stand a chance.

"For your grandmother it was the right thing for you to do," Yvonne's mother said. "No harm done; besides, it might work."

The voice of the Arnolds.

The old wanted her to win.

That included Truston.

As for the young, that was another story.

Including her. The mysterious Y.

Emilie brought home the North Kingstown High School yearbook. "I think she's as pretty as you are." She pointed to this year's Prettiest Girl, Beverly Donovan. "This picture isn't as pretty as she really is, you should see her in person."

"I remember her, she's pretty."

How pretty was her grandmother? How pretty was her other grandmother?

Which one of them had been prettier?

XI

"You can't ever learn if you're afraid to fall," Mrs. Coyle said angrily, after Yvonne had been practicing at camp for a week. "Everybody falls sometimes. Just make sure you fall on your fanny. Have you been doing the back arches?"

Yvonne couldn't do them in her cabin room. The floor was splintery. The only comfortable place was out on the grass by the flagpole, in the late afternoon before the mosquitoes came out and after the sun had eased a little. Up on a little mound, far enough away so that if anyone really wanted to gawk they had to come up close, an intrusion. Nobody dared. "We've got to give Miss Rhode Island some privacy," Mrs. Coyle had said at the first camp assembly. "We've got to let her practice. You girls going into competition know how important that is."

When all the girls looked directly at her, Yvonne knew she'd made a mistake: She should have gone to a figure-skating school instead of to skating camp.

"I always do my exercises. An hour a day. Even before I came to camp. But I'm afraid I'll break my arm again."

"You can't be chicken. You have to take the risk."

"Maybe I shouldn't do the layback spin."

But the layback spin is the one audiences like most,

that's the crowd pleaser, that's what makes them happy, when the skater is going around, almost off balance, back arched, face up, hips forward, that's what really turns them on.

But who can do it?

Maybe Yvonne couldn't.

"Maybe I should be happy with the sit spin. It's hard but I can do it. Maybe I should just practice my routine. I don't have it yet. I've got to pick the music."

"Heel down," Mrs. Coyle said briskly. "Don't forget to keep the heel pushed down on every spin."

Yvonne broke away and began skating. Into the sit spin. Back crossover. First, second, third, fourth crossover, easy. Free leg out, easy. Slow squat, steady, control the wobble, hold the free leg, not so easy, a grunt, no grunting in Atlantic City, hands below the knee, arm hooked around the skating leg: the sit spin. Eight revolutions, without getting dizzy.

"It's hard to go down and then get up out of that."

"Press your hand on your knee to get up. Just one hand. Hold on to your leg with your other hand. You're not ready for both hands yet."

The champions train three hours a day.

Yvonne would work four.

Two in the morning. Two in the afternoon. Plus an hour of exercises. Two hours on parts of the routine. One hour individual practice. One hour late in the afternoon picking up on individual problems.

Sudo, I sweat. *Celerissima,* swiftest (female).

When raising and lowering the body, don't think about balancing, just balance.

Equilibrium, a Latin word? What declension?

After the first three weeks, another hour of practice had to be added: the entire routine.

161

But for the routine she needed to select the music.

It ought to be fast for the spins and slow for the spirals. "Remember," Mrs. Melli had said, "whatever you choose is going to sound different at the pageant. The record you practice to has a big orchestra. The pageant only has a band."

"How about 'Try Not to Worry'?" A nice selection for a girl who had broken her arm. "That's both fast and slow."

"Copyright." Mrs. Melli sounded very firm. "It costs money. Make sure you get something old. Get classical."

"You can always do *Carmen*," Mrs. Coyle said. She put her hand on the small of Yvonne's back. "Straighter!"

"What tune?"

Mrs. Coyle sang it. As she sang, her shoulders began twitching from side to side, she was off on the ice, the routine was being formed, a forward spiral, three cross-overs, a little one-foot spin, out of the spin, da, dum dum dum, a bunny hop. "Get it?" Mrs. Coyle said as she skated back to Yvonne's side.

"The music is so square. I hate it."

"But it makes your bottom bump out every time. You can't skate to that without a good wiggle. It shows off your figure."

"*Carmen* is good," Mrs. Melli said over the phone that night. "I'm going to call Atlantic City first thing tomorrow. They like a little variety, but it's good to have some old favorites, it's good, it keeps you at the right level. They hear Wellesley, they're going to think you chose Beethoven, but when they hear *Carmen* that's good, it will make everybody feel comfortable. I like the great themes."

Yvonne knew it; it meant she would lose. Girls with

162

Carmen didn't win, girls with *Madame Butterfly.* "I don't want it, I think it's cheap."

"You're the final judge, you have to do what you feel comfortable with. I'm not running the show, I'm just here to make sure you're not sorry in the end."

"I'll think of something."

Handel: the *Water Music.*

"What's that?" Mrs. Coyle said when Yvonne told her. "This is ice, not water."

They had to drive to the public library in St. Johnsbury to borrow a record they could listen to.

"Perfect," Mrs. Coyle said when she heard it. "I'm going to call up Mrs. Melli and tell her so myself."

"Go out and buy the record," Yvonne said to Mrs. Melli. "You can get it at the Warwick Mall."

"I know where to buy a record."

"When you get it play the last band, the last section on the second side, that's it."

The next day Yvonne was having lunch in the dining room—it was hard to diet on these lunches, but they had fresh vegetables, butter beans, zucchini, good cucumbers—when the camp nurse came in and called her to the telephone.

"I think it's terrific," Mrs. Melli said. "I bought it this morning, it's perfect. I think you can win with it. It's got class."

"Mail me the record," Yvonne told Mrs. Melli. "We can't keep the library copy out too long."

Two days later two copies came in separate packages, by registered mail.

For Mrs. Melli no effort was too great.

"I'm not working hard enough," Yvonne said one day

163

when she saw Mrs. Coyle coming into the rink to spend her hour.

"I think you're working hard. You just have to keep remembering the tips I give you."

"If I was working harder, it wouldn't be so tough to stand up after a sit spin. Every time I do it I think I'm going to fall. I'm afraid I'll fall when I do my talent." Just standing still on her skates Yvonne began to wobble a little bit.

"Keep working, you'll get it."

"Don't get discouraged." Mrs. Melli called again that night. "I bet you're discouraged up there all alone with nothing but those little kids and that Mrs. Coyle. She's nice, but she can't really understand what you're going through, I know how you feel."

"I'm all right." But there was no place to talk privately. The phone was in the camp nurse's office. Usually the nurse sat in the next room listening, that was the infirmary, there was always somebody there. Would it be Yvonne there soon, with a broken arm again?

"In two weeks you'll have it down cold, maybe you don't have to stay the whole time."

"But we paid for it already."

"I'll come up visiting day with your parents. In the same car."

The ride up alone could convince you. Vermont and New Hampshire, both of them are more beautiful than Rhode Island. Once you get up past Concord, there's nothing but mountains all the way.

"What a beautiful ride up," Yvonne's mother said. "I never realized New Hampshire was so pretty."

"I didn't think so," Yvonne said. It had been rainy the day they delivered her to camp. Now it was sunny. "I'll take Rhode Island any day."

164

"You look beautiful."

Her father remembered.

"I don't feel it. I spend all my time sweating and the showers here aren't private, they have canvas walls, they have outdoor showers." Yvonne shivered. "You have to make sure you don't get splinters in your feet. If I got a splinter, it would kill me, it would waste a week's skating time. It could get infected. I might not even be able to walk right."

Up and down the runway.

"We brought up a cake for you."

Her mother remembered too.

"I'm trying to diet. The food's fattening here. They think you get rid of it by exercising, but I don't. I can't eat cucumbers all the time."

"Yvonne," Mrs. Melli's voice sounded strangled. "I can see it in your fanny."

Who was it who blushed? Not Yvonne, but her mother.

"Throw away that damn cake. Flush it. I'll take it home with me myself."

"What kind is it?" Yvonne dared to ask.

"Never mind." Her mother was too frightened to tell.

"You don't eat for two days." Mrs. Melli was now in charge. "You just don't put anything in your damn mouth. I don't care if you fall down from hunger, you just don't eat."

"That's not a healthy way to diet." Now Yvonne's mother was angry, watching out for her child's health.

"I don't give a damn, you just don't let anything into your mouth, don't even brush your teeth. That happens all the time, they get so nervous they eat, some of them do it right at Atlantic City. They go into a beauty contest, Miss America, and they gain five pounds, three, four pounds right there. One girl, she gained five pounds. Or

165

they diet too much and end up too damn skinny. You got to nip it in the bud. You just don't eat nothing for two days. Then you go on a good diet. I better get into a motel room around here. Maybe they can put me up at camp, you don't know how to take care of yourself."

Even off ice skates, Mrs. Coyle seemed to glide. She came up to them. "How do you like our little champion now?"

"She's fat, you got to do something about the damn food you serve here. I'm going to get into your kitchen and make her some salads. Do you have any cottage cheese? Not today, but tomorrow."

"You told me you had the right kind of food here." Yvonne's father zooming in, a hockey stick.

"It is good." Now even Yvonne's head felt heavy. "That's how I gained weight. I'll take it off. Stop nagging at me, for God's sakes. Everybody's after me. All the time. I'll just taste the frosting, only a little bit. Then take it away, you eat."

"You're making a big mistake, Yvonne." Mrs. Melli spoke very slowly.

"You can trust me. Why don't you trust me?" Miss Rhode Island, great-hipped.

"Let's see you skate." A feint by Mrs. Melli.

Chocolate. Yvonne dipped her finger into the frosting and took a taste.

"Delicious," she said. "I can't skate now. They're having an exhibition for the parents. I'll be in that."

"We wanted her to be the star. We've got her featured. The parents will love it, Miss Rhode Island. The problem is this, a lot of the girls are better skaters."

"I can't do a layback spin. I still wobble a little on the sit spin."

166

"Your sit spin is fine. You might feel like you wobble but you can hardly see it."

"I'm sure you're wonderful, dear." Mrs. Melli was still hard at work. "I think she's a winner."

"Didn't you see me wobble? Just a little bit?" Yvonne said to her mother after the show. "Wasn't it evident?"

"Just a little bit."

"What are they talking about to say I don't wobble any?"

"They're trying to keep you in good spirits."

"With lies?"

"They have a job to do, so they're doing it."

"They're doing a job on me. I hate it."

"When I lost it, I didn't have any qualms about it." Mrs. Melli held her hand to her midriff. Which breast was the artificial one? Mrs. Melli was big-busted.

"It must have been very frightening."

"I didn't worry for me, I felt bad for my husband. It always meant a lot to him, you know what I mean."

A week after visiting day and Mrs. Melli was back. For one last look at Yvonne's talent. "Your boyfriend, what's his name, he'll know what I mean."

"I'm not seeing him anymore."

"What happened? Don't tell me you got smart!"

Mrs. Melli was drinking vodka and tonic. Yvonne a Diet Pepsi. Before answering, she took a sip.

"We decided to break up."

"There's still calories in that, it says diet, but that don't mean it's got no calories. You should have something with absolutely no calories, maybe one calorie per serving, soda water with lime in it, you should try that. What are you going to do, you need a boyfriend."

"I'm sure I can get one." Yvonne's hand closed around the glass. Now it had Miss Rhode Island's fingerprints on it.

"They'll ask you, the judges want to know, do you have a boyfriend? You have to have one. If you don't they think you're some kind of freak, a lesbian."

"You shouldn't attack lesbians, that's their sexual persuasion."

"Don't give me lib talk like that." For this, Mrs. Melli had to take another swallow of her drink. "I can't stand it, don't say that to the judges. Say, that's a terrible problem, if they ask you. Say, I feel sorry for them. You got to have a name. They ask you about your boyfriend, you got to name someone, not that one from Harvard either."

"I'll sneak in my brother. I can make up something about him, they won't know."

"That's crazy. They should have picked that colored girl. What was her name? Nelda. What a name! They have such unusual names. Unusual names help, sometimes I think that. They had two Miss Americas named Bebe. It's time for a colored to win anyway. Don't you have any boy you could invite down? Just for one day? The final party? You don't have to spend much time with him. That's your boyfriend." The restaurant waiter was a college boy, but homely, too skinny. Mrs. Melli beckoned to him. "I'll take another one of these."

"I could ask Arthur Poulos." Yvonne held up her glass to the waiter too.

"Don't get her Diet Pepsi."

The waiter looked at Yvonne for a decision.

"That's the kind I like."

"O.K., you got a craving, are you pregnant? That's all

168

we need. Go ahead, get it for her, drink it, go to the dogs, it doesn't matter anyway. Who's this Poulos?"

"He's somebody I know. He goes to medical school."

"Is he good-looking?"

The answer: Yvonne smiled.

"Is he from Rhode Island?"

"Narragansett Pier."

"Invite him. He doesn't go to Harvard, does he?"

"B.U."

"I'll talk to him, I'll tell him what to do. You tell him to call me up. Just don't go ice skating with this one. No accidents, you know what I mean. You practicing your skating?"

"I'm still worried about it."

"Don't worry about it, the Talent doesn't count so much. It isn't so important as Swimsuit, Swimsuit's always been the most important, Swimsuit and General Personality. You drink that all the way down, you're going to ruin yourself for Swimsuit." The waiter had put the glass of Diet Pepsi down in front of Yvonne.

"I don't have the layback spin right, yet. Maybe I'll leave it out. But I'm good on the one-foot, I'll show it to you tomorrow, with the music."

The music.

Yvonne, spinning.

Torso forward. That torso, the slender rib cage, the soft shoulders. The hair streams around, ice blond, the arms extend, reaching out toward the planets Venus and Jupiter, the world turns.

The layback spin: the breasts up toward the heavens, facing the light from the sun, the moon.

"I think that's just beautiful." Mrs. Melli stood outside

169

the rink with Mrs. Coyle. "That's all the talent she needs. Too much is not good sometimes."

"Keep your back straighter, Yvonne." Without her ice skates on Mrs. Coyle always talked softly. "Make sure your shoulders are even."

"Are my legs getting big from so much skating?"

Mrs. Melli crouched down to look. Her eyes were at Yvonne's knee level. "You better stop as soon as the pageant is over. It looks ugly when they get too many muscles, that's why dancers never win, did you ever notice?"

Outside the rink, heat. Mountain heat, suitable for mosquitoes. When it gets hot up there, there's no ocean to cool it off. "It must have been terrible driving up here in this heat." Breastless.

"Don't feel sorry for me. I got air conditioning in the car."

All over America, heat. Perhaps not for Miss Alaska, perhaps not for Miss Hawaii. But in Arizona, Miss Arizona stayed indoors. In Texas, Miss Texas walked naked in her room. In Evanston, Miss Illinois lay on the grass in the shade. Think of them, all of them, sweet-scented, sweat drops beginning to form. All their sprays, all their roll-ons dissolved by the heat.

"Hello, Miss Rhode Island." A little blond girl walking by greeted Yvonne.

"Cute little girl," Mrs. Melli said. "I looked over all the girls here, you're the best."

"I'm not always the prettiest. There's some pretty girls here."

"You've got to stop thinking like that. You're the prettiest in Rhode Island. Maybe in the whole country."

With a sweaty back.

"I need a shower." Outside the rink there was a bench

under a pine tree. "Let's sit down here. Maybe it's cooler."

"Don't you ever think about being Miss America? That's what you're supposed to do. Don't you think what you'll do with your sixty thousand dollars if you win?"

"I know what I'd do, I'd buy land."

I'd never ice-skate again. I'd never fall down. I'd never break my arm.

"That's a funny thing for a girl to say."

"In Rhode Island, right on the bay. Or maybe Block Island, maybe Charlestown. I'd put up a big wooden fence, those fences made out of poles stuck close together, not the kind you can see through. And I'd plant food there and put up a little house. I'd be self-sufficient."

"That's weird."

"Maybe after a while I'd invite you down to have a look."

"When are you going to call up this Pollo? Is he an Italian boy?"

"I'd plant what the Indians planted, the three sisters, corn, beans, and squash. I'd eat clams from the beach. I'd go fishing. I'd live just like the Indians lived. I'd drop out of school for a year. If I wanted to take courses I'd drive over to Kingston to the university."

"What about Pollo?"

"Poulos. He's Greek."

"You call him tonight. I'm not leaving Vermont until you call him."

Poulos, your time is coming. Aphrodite hovers over you. Priapos will whisper in your ear.

"What's his first name?"

"Arthur. I can call him at medical school, they go to school during the summer."

"Maybe I can get the newspaper to do the article about him too." Mrs. Melli got up, she shook out her skirt where it was sticking to her in the heat, she gave a subtle hitch to her bra strap, was that the side holding up the artificial breast?

"How can the newspaper write anything? There's nothing to write."

"They always do a big feature on you in the summer right before the pageant."

Poulos in a bathing suit, going down the walkway. The bathing suit, tight, flame red, short but decently so, his build the best in sight, perhaps the best on Narragansett Beach, perhaps in Rhode Island.

He moved slowly, wouldn't you know he was certain he was gorgeous, very Grecian. The walkway went over the sands, the sands sloped down to the sea, the sea washed away from Rhode Island, tide out, going all around the earth. Goddesses, are you swimming? Is Poulos really the one?

Yvonne walked behind. Poulos knew Narragansett, he came from the town, this was his beach, he would pick the site.

In its own way, Narragansett Beach is as beautiful as Moonstone. The light is different, more alert.

In that light, Poulos's shoulders, Poulos's long legs. Think of them in a white room on the East Side of Providence, hour after hour, while his nurse sends patients in to him one by one. They would take off their clothes. He would touch.

"Are you enjoying the summer?"

Poulos spread out the enormous beach towel. On it was a picture of a dollar bill. "I'm delivering babies. I

172

have to be back there by midnight. So far two little black baby girls."

"Maybe one of them will be Miss America someday." By handing Poulos the suntan lotion, Yvonne was saying: Spread me. All the queens, of California, of Carolina, knew what this gesture meant.

"How do you like being Miss Rhode Island?"

"I'm not enjoying it." To help the spreading, Yvonne, lying down on her belly, unhitched the back of her bathing-suit bra. "I have to get a better tan. I have to practice skating. I can't eat too much. I'm getting nervous. I find I'm forgetting my Latin, I can't even remember what some words mean, school is so far away."

The pressure of Poulos's hands, pleasant or unpleasant?

"Sometimes I think I'm going to win, sometimes I think I'm going to lose."

Pleasant.

"But I want to win."

"You have a good tan already." Poulos's bathing suit, was it getting even tighter?

Maybe at Atlantic City Poulos would win.

"I have a good talent. I have a good figure. I have a good personality. That's still no guarantee I'm going to win. Sixty thousand dollars, that's what I get if I win, maybe seventy. Applause makes me nervous."

"You might get used to it."

"Can you do my legs? I have good legs." Who could doubt it? "Sometimes I think it's true what everybody says, they sleep with the judges, that's how they win." Hook up the bra. "But I didn't sleep with anyone for Miss Rhode Island. I won anyway. I guess it's fate. But I won because I go to Wellesley. That's my talent, Latin,

173

but now I'm forgetting it. How would you like to be in a beauty contest?"

Poulos of the white teeth, Mr. Shoulders. It was good not to have been a body builder and still have a strong body anyway. It looked handsomer. He didn't need suntan lotion. So what! Yvonne put some on his back anyway.

"I got into medical school. That was enough for me."

Ahead, Narragansett Bay. Blue. Behind, Rhode Island. Green. Would that be enough for you?

"Well, I have to go through with it, I can't quit now. Will you come down to Atlantic City to cheer me on?"

"I'll still be delivering babies."

"Can't you switch with someone? I'd like you to come to the Coronation Ball if I'm crowned." On this beach, real surf, loud and ominous. If Poulos said no, she would lose. "Even if I'm not crowned." On this beach there were smooth white stones like those on Moonstone, egg-shaped, but not so large. Yvonne took one and threw it —no, cast it deliberately—toward the waves.

Poulos held a handful of sand; it trickled out slowly like sand in an hourglass. Poulos at his coronation. In his bathing suit. Pivoting around, his hands wave above his head, back and forth, an Olympic champion. Upon his head, a crown; it sits easily on the curls. Each crashing of the ocean waves, a surge of applause.

"Yes or no?"

"Sure, I'll arrange to switch with someone."

So now he had to chase Yvonne. Swift as a seabird diving, she was running down to the water.

Most beautiful. Most likely to succeed. But here at least, not fastest.

Poulos was faster, Poulos reached her, Poulos

174

swooped one arm around her waist, the other behind her knees, swung her up into his arms, carried her toward the water.

Romantique.

Poulos's task: to bear her into the water and drop her in.

Yvonne's task: to kick her feet in mock terror, to wriggle slightly, but not enough to make him lose his balance, to shriek.

Have you ever picked up the girl and run with her toward the water?

Have you ever been lifted up and carried down to be immersed in a great ocean by the powerful one?

Only the strongest boys dare try it—and on whom?— on only the prettiest girls, on only those whose little cries go out toward the goddess, sharp little cries, tender, promising the great cry later, the great shriek, you can hear it sometimes as the waves crash on the beach.

Are you eligible?

You've seen them do it, the youths in their bright, glistening suits. You've heard the screams and the low roaring sound of the boys as they run swiftly toward the water and seen the bright drops of ocean water fall, shaken off their legs as they run again up onto the beach.

Perhaps in Atlantic City, there, the great He will lift up each of the girls, all of the princesses, and run roaring with them into the waves. There they will be cast into the sea—once they came out of it—and hold court in the green palace underneath, swaying their arms back and forth like sea plants sending waves of praise toward her, the sea queen, Miss Ocean State.

Glistening sea drops scattered. Yvonne was shaking

175

her hair. She patted the wetness off the bottom of her bathing suit. Poulos was wet too. He had fallen down with her into the waves. "If I get crowned," she said, "you have to have the first dance with me."

XII

"Ladies and gentlemen!" A clanging on the side of a ginger-ale bottle, the bell of destiny. Representative Ashkenazy, the head of the committee, was beginning his speech.

"This year we've got a winner. I can feel it. It's a great year for Rhode Island. All the work Mrs. Melli has done over the years. This fine young lady. Her fine family."

Yvonne's ankles for the skating, her feet. Yvonne's breasts for the Swimsuit. Yvonne's smile for the interview with the judges.

"Look at her. She will make us all proud."

"I am proud of you," her mother said. "Aren't I, Emilie?"

But Emilie didn't answer.

Miss Rhode Island's mother wore a pale yellow summer dress, below the knee, an almost invisible print on it, white butterflies. Scoop collar. Medium heels. A corsage of yellow roses.

Miss Rhode Island's sister: a pink and white candy-striped skinny jumper, acetate, shirred at the waist, with a white blouse. A gardenia.

Miss Rhode Island's brother and father: plaid summer trousers, blue for Joseph, red for his father, and matching solid-color summerweight jackets. Joseph was actually wearing a necktie. Like his father.

All of it new. The corsages, a gift of the committee. The rest of it $325, more or less.

Emilie in a room with her grandmother. $35 a day with breakfast. Joseph sharing with Poulos, only $17.50. Hotel total: $92.50 a day, plus tax. But it was a wonderful occasion.

"Let me pay you for what it costs to come down here, I know it's expensive." Yvonne made the offer to her mother because her father would automatically say no. "Out of my winnings."

What would your mother say? What would your father? "That's your money, dear. We wouldn't touch it." That's what they would say, right? Wouldn't they?

"All they think about is money, the other girls." Yvonne couldn't talk to Poulos unless Mrs. Melli was around, but Mrs. Melli was halfway across the room, busy talking to another Rhode Islander, a young-looking thin woman, maybe she had once been a contestant herself. "You know what the one from New Jersey said to me— I knew she was from New Jersey, we all have little badges with the name and the state on them, they're shaped like hearts—you know what she said, 'I'm only in it for the cash.' I'm sure she'll lose, maybe they ought to put our telephone numbers on the badges for movie scouts."

"You don't want to be in the movies," Poulos said.

But maybe he was wrong. Maybe he could be in the movies with her.

Mrs. Melli was looking. "How'm I doing?" Yvonne smiled prettily at her.

"You look lovely."

True, nobody else in the room was as pretty.

But there were no judges in the room.

The night of the state welcomes, the judges might be having their own party. Or maybe they got together every evening after the judging to laugh at the girls.

It was too serious for laughing.

"You'll do just beautiful, you mustn't stay just with him." Mrs. Melli edged Poulos aside and put her arm around Yvonne. "These are the people who paid for your car."

A kiss to Representative Ashkenazy.

"Remember, I'm the chaperone here, watch out. I should get to kiss him too."

The representative, a big-handed, red-haired man, put his arm around Mrs. Melli, and kissed her too.

When somebody else, from the Chamber of Commerce, Providence, came up, a slow-moving man with heavy lips and a cigar, Yvonne knew what to do. "I'd love to kiss you, cross my heart. But you have to kiss my chaperone first."

A scream of laughter from Mrs. Melli. She already had three drinks in her. "You got to watch this girl. I think she's really going to win."

O Goddess, hovering over the shores of the Atlantic, over the high room where the Rhode Islanders meet, grant her wish.

"I can kiss her little sister." This from Mr. Douro, Mrs. Melli's next-door neighbor. He came down every year. He giggled with excitement, a little man, Portuguese, his bald head well tanned. But there was Doucette suddenly in the way, his arm around Emilie.

This year Mr. Melli hadn't come. He had gone fishing off Block Island, a three-day trip.

"I am proud to represent Rhode Island," Yvonne said to Representative Ashkenazy. Behind her back Joseph came up to her, he grabbed her hand, abruptly raised her

179

arm. "The winner," he said. Very forceful. He was as strong as Poulos, Maybe he was stronger than Representative Ashkenazy. Yvonne let out a squeal, a gasp, the queen surprised by one of her courtiers.

"Watch out, Yvonne." Mrs. Melli, like her dogs, was always on guard. "I'm chaperoning you."

"I'm only her brother."

But Mrs. Melli already knew that.

"You're a male."

"That's no lie." Joseph put his arm around Mrs. Melli. Maybe he's the one who would be the politician. Senator Doucette.

"You take care of her"—Yvonne poked Joseph with her finger—"while I go off and flirt with the men." Was this what it means: She's in her element? Was this her element? Not just her element. Everybody's? Like being the bride at the wedding party, with a hundred grooms dancing around her.

Walking on jetties, that's my favorite kind of walking. We have nice trails in the woods. We have some historic routes, the hill in Providence. But I love it best walking out on jetties, those big piles of rocks out into the middle of the water. We have one in Rhode Island, it's a half mile long, you have to jump from rock to rock, it's got a little lighthouse out at the end, yes, I love to walk.

That one scored perhaps. It's good for the energy crisis to have a Miss America who loves to walk.

And what other sports do you take part in?

The judges are judging. Jetties weren't enough.

Oh, I play tennis. I like sailing. I've crewed in some races. We do a lot of sailing in Rhode Island, it's a big thing and it's not just the yacht-club people. I swim a lot in the summertime. And I skate, skating's my talent.

What kind of music do you like?

I play the piano, mostly for fun. I play piano pieces, not whole sonatas, Chopin, stuff like that.

Who's your favorite rock group?

A tricky question. It could be the key. It has to be a refined rock group, not too kinky. It has to be middle, but not square. There is a right rock group, which is it?

I don't like rock music that much. I enjoy dancing to it, I like to listen as background sometimes, but I don't follow them.

Was there consternation in the air? Was there a rock musician on the panel of judges?

Isn't there anyone you like a lot?

Yes, the Stones. Sometimes the Mothers.

No points on that, that was a loss.

How about schooling? What do you like best in school? What's your ambition?

I'm going to be a professor. You can do that and still raise a family. I'm going to teach Latin. That's my major, Latin.

If you had one period of history to choose from to go back to, which period would you choose?

I'd choose the time of the settlement of Rhode Island by Roger Williams and Anne Hutchinson and the Arnolds. That's who I'm descended from, the Arnolds. I'd choose 1686, when the French first came to live in Rhode Island, in North Kingstown. That's the town I live in. I'd choose the time when the woods weren't cut down yet and I'd spend every night sleeping out under the trees.

I'd choose a hundred years from now. If we can go back, why can't we go forward? I'd choose the time when apartment houses line Narragansett Bay from Providence to Point Judith, and they're all filled with people, millions of them, since the population has exploded, and they look out the windows toward the bay; and I'm drawn down the bay on water skis, with one hand waving to them; and none of them, not one, is as beautiful as I am, neither there nor on the other shore going back up the bay along the East Passage from Newport up to East Providence, and up the Seekonk River as far as Pawtucket.

I'd choose the time before the Indians came. The time after the glacier had melted. When the land was bare, before the plants and the people were there. And I'd climb up a hill to look out over the islands and over the stone fields, and I'd turn from north to south and then north again, and I'd call out, "Here I am! Miss Rhode Island!"

And how are you serving your community?

By being Miss Rhode Island, by being beautiful, by restricting my caloric intake, by appearing pleased when people smile at me, by coming to Atlantic City, by wearing a swimsuit.

And what is your ambition?

To be beautiful, to be as beautiful as the goddess is beautiful, to drive men insane with desire and fear and women insane with rage.

And who is your favorite singer? What is your favorite music?

My favorite music hasn't been written yet, but I hear it anyway. My favorite singer is the blind man who sings about my beauty.

What is your favorite food?

The heart.

Are you a Democrat or a Republican? What is your favorite animal?

The governor, the mayor.

These are the answers.

What do you think of women's lib?

Yvonne's strange cry! Yvonne's shrieking! It frightens the judges. But it is the right answer.

"I'm supposed to screen all messages. Seven thirty-two." Mrs. Melli called out the room number to the desk clerk. "Mash notes, there's always a couple of those, from perfect strangers. I have to answer the phone in the room, don't you pick it up, Yvonne."

"How would a stranger know what room I'm in, it doesn't make sense. I think the way we're closed off here is silly. I might as well go up to the room if I can't see the messages." Yvonne began to walk away toward the elevator.

"Hold off." Mrs. Melli was reaching over to pick up some pieces of paper from the desk clerk. "Wait for me, I'm coming right with you. You aren't supposed to go up alone, you know that."

"What are those papers?"

"Give me a chance to look. One year there was this pervert, he sent the same dirty letter to every one of the girls. That was before my time, but they still talk about it, there's nothing here."

"Of course there's something there. He gave you some papers, didn't he?"

"Here comes an elevator." With her hand pushing Yvonne's back, Mrs. Melli headed across the lobby. "It's nothing, they ask for interviews, that kind of thing. It's none of your business, you got to think about the show, you got Swimsuit tomorrow, think about that. You don't have free time for interviews, hello, how are you, dear."

Miss Illinois was in the elevator already, along with her chaperone.

"Don't she look pretty, Yvonne?"

"I love your dress." Yvonne smiled, showing teeth. "It looks washable too." She pressed the seven button. Twelve was already lighted, nine, fourteen. Miss Illinois had been given a higher number than Miss Rhode Island. "How do you keep looking so good? I'm bushed, I must look awful. I just want to take my shoes off. I didn't know it took so much standing around just to get a TV show ready. I'm going to make sure I wear low heels tomorrow."

"I just loved it. You don't look tired at all. I love rehearsing almost as much as performance. My aim is to go into the legitimate theater."

The doors opened, seven. Everybody else in the elevator, even Mrs. Melli, shrank back to allow Miss Rhode Island to get out. Her stop.

"I want to know what the messages are. They're for me, aren't they, not for you."

"When we get in the room."

Inside the room, Mrs. Melli ripped open an envelope.

"It's nothing. Nothing important." She opened her pocketbook and put the paper inside.

"It's from Truston, I can tell."

No answer.

Mrs. Melli went over to the air-conditioning unit and snapped it on. She twisted the knob. "Hi-kool, I think I got it."

"What does the letter say?"

Mrs. Melli dragged a vinyl armchair close to the bed so she could put her feet up. "He wants to see you." She leaned down and took off her shoes. "He's even staying in this hotel, he got a room here."

"How did he know where I was?"

"They list it. There's seven good hotels here. They have a press release saying where every state is."

184

"I don't know if I should see him." Yvonne went over to the window and looked out. The room faced north. Out across the water, Moonstone Beach. "Maybe I shouldn't."

"Maybe?" Mrs. Melli raised her voice. "Maybe? Are you cracked? You shouldn't go near him, he's poison. He's going to hang around the lobby, he's going to wait by the elevator until you go by. Did you know he was going to come down here?"

"No." Yvonne got up to go toward the bathroom. "But I'm not surprised."

"I'm not surprised either." Mrs. Melli got up to follow Yvonne; after the bathroom door was closed she stood outside it. She banged on the door with her hand. "I'm not surprised. Do you think I'm stupid?"

She was still standing there when Yvonne opened the door to come out.

"I know I shouldn't see him." Yvonne walked past Mrs. Melli and over to her bed. "It's wrong to see him now, he can wait a few days."

"Don't worry, he won't even want to see you in a few days if you don't get to be Miss America. You listen to me, if you win, you'll see him again; if not, you got nothing to worry about. What are you doing?" Mrs. Melli's voice rose, a storm wind. "What the hell are you doing?"

She rushed over to try to grab the telephone out of Yvonne's hand.

"Could you connect me with Truston Clapp, I don't know his room number."

"Put down the phone, Yvonne."

"I told you I don't know his room number."

Mrs. Melli's fist slammed down. Cut off.

"Give me the phone."

185

"Look, you're not going to stop me."

"It's against the rules. You get bounced. You can't talk to anybody without me, you know that."

"I don't mind talking in front of you." Yvonne handed Mrs. Melli the receiver. "You call him, set up a time."

"You think I'm crazy, I'm not going to do that." Mrs. Melli clutched the phone, she held it to her breast.

"I'll call him if you won't. I'll wait till you're asleep."

"You have to go to sleep early, you can't stay up late, you need to get your rest. I'll call him. But don't think I'm going to let you get near him. What the hell does he want anyway, why is he here? He's a stupid one." Mrs. Melli dialed the operator. "He's a real bastard, Truston Clapp, I don't know his room number. I never had something like this before. Will you connect me? See, it's ringing, he's not there, he must have left, maybe he had the brains to cut out, he must have thought better of it, hello, is this Mr. Clapp?"

"Have you got him?"

"Watch out." Mrs. Melli spoke in a low voice. "This is Mrs. Melli, Yvonne's chaperone. Look, we can have you kicked out of the hotel, I can arrange that. Nobody's supposed to molest the girls. I think you better leave. I can get the police, you know the Atlantic City Police Department don't want any old men molesting the girls."

"ROOM SEVEN THIRTY-TWO, TRUSTON!" A howl from Miss Rhode Island. It went over the sound of the air conditioner, out into the hall, out past the window glass. "SEVEN THIRTY-TWO!"

Mrs. Melli hung up.

"If he knocks on the door, I'm going to get the cops."

"It will get into the newspapers."

186

"At this point, I don't give a damn."

"I bet the other girls would back me. I don't want to go to bed with him, I don't even want to see him that much, remember, I've got Arthur here. But he makes the effort to come all the way down here from Providence, it's just a courtesy to talk to him. He didn't come to the Rhode Island party. Maybe he's here with his wife. You know, you were never fair to him, I'm not in love with him. I don't think it helps my appearance, I mean physically, to have a scene. I don't think we should have yelling, that kind of scene, the cops at the door. I don't see what you're making such a fuss about. There he is now."

First the knock. Then, in a low voice, "Yvonne."

Mrs. Melli opened the door just a little. Then she closed it fast, right behind him.

"How do you do, Mrs. Melli. I've heard a lot about you." Truston looked relaxed. He was wearing all white; he seemed as tanned as Miss California, the only color on him: a small green alligator emblem on his shirt. He put out his hand.

Mrs. Melli didn't put hers out, though.

"You should be ashamed of yourself chasing somebody like her. You should go after old ladies, not college girls. What about your wife? You're a disgrace. How old are you anyway?"

From the way she looked him over, it was clear Mrs. Melli thought he was attractive.

"I just wanted to give our girl here a good-luck kiss." Truston sat down on the bed, he spread his palm flat and moved it back and forth over the bedspread that had covered Yvonne at night. How did he know? He picked the right one, Yvonne's, not the bed Mrs. Melli had slept in. "Now take it easy. I'm not so old. We're probably the

187

same age, Mrs. Melli, but you look ten years younger. Maybe I ought to take you out for a drink. We could have a talk."

Mrs. Melli sat down again in the vinyl armchair, she groped on the floor for her shoes. No clothes off with this one around.

"Why did you come, Truston?" Yvonne sat primly in a straight-backed chair by the desk. "I thought you weren't going to come. I thought you were going to watch it on TV. I thought you'd be down at the beach with your family. How come you got away from your wife?"

"Yes, how come?" Mrs. Melli had both her shoes on now. "What the hell are you doing here anyway?"

"I needed to see you. I had to touch you. For luck." He put his hand out toward Yvonne. "I wanted to make sure you win."

Whose luck, his or hers? His obviously. Yvonne knew.

"I'm not supposed to be alone with you. I can't go away from Mrs. Melli. You know that."

"I don't mind if she watches."

"You pig!" Mrs. Melli stood up, she leaned over the bed, she was almost touching Truston. "You're disgusting. Get him out of here, Yvonne, now do you see what kind of person he is? You don't need that kind of talk, it's going to affect your looks, he's killing you."

"Don't get so agitated." Truston's big hand, held up. The fingers spread wide. Halt! If he moved a little way forward, he would be feeling Mrs. Melli's breast. "What could make her look prettier than spending a little time with me?"

Private time?

"Truston, you have to give me one good-luck kiss and then you have to go away." Yvonne got up off her chair and began walking toward him. "Just a kiss."

188

"This one won't stop with just a kiss." Mrs. Melli began to hurry around to the other side of the bed.

"Don't worry. You'll do what I say, right, Truston?"

Truston got up off the bed.

"Just a kiss, Truston."

He went over to where Yvonne was standing. Mrs. Melli moved back to lean against the closet door, she held on to the closet doorknob. "Just a kiss now," she said. "Don't do nothing else."

But Yvonne put her arms up, they went around Truston's neck. Her thighs pressed against his. One of his hands roamed her back, the other hand reached, grabbed lower, his leg pushed against her, between her legs; their mouths were together, their tongues.

Not exactly what you would call "just a kiss."

Mrs. Melli's silence: Was it only the silence of guilt, the shame of the neglectful chaperone?

"Stop it!" Finally she hissed at them. "Stop it!" But it didn't work. "Stop it, for Christ's sake!"

Weren't they going to stop?

"Stop it!" Loud, you could hear it. "Stop it!" Louder. Drumming.

There was a sudden dreadful knocking on the door of the room.

Quickly, Yvonne pulled herself away from Truston. Back to the safety of the desk chair, with Truston still standing there in the middle of the room big as life. Actually bigger, if you happened to be looking front and center, below the waistline.

Another thundering knock. Mrs. Melli narrowed her eyes almost shut and turned around swiftly to face the closet door.

It hadn't been just imagination, a terrible fantasy. They were all totally silent.

189

Even so, the knocking came again, loud, astonishing.

It made Truston tiptoe away from the center of the room over to the vinyl chair. He sat down. That way he didn't stand out quite so shamefully.

"We have to answer it," Mrs. Melli whispered.

"Why?" Yvonne ran her hand over her hair. It was neat.

The judges, doing an on-site inspection? The TV sponsors?

"They know we're up here." Mrs. Melli went over to the door. "Who is it out there?" She spoke in a low voice. "Don't you know you're supposed to telephone from downstairs?"

"It's Joseph Doucette."

Yvonne jumped up and ran over to the door. "Joseph, what are you doing here?"

"I have to talk to you."

"Can't you come back later?" Mrs. Melli spoke in her normal loud voice.

"Open up, will you, Yvonne."

"I can't, I'm busy now."

"Listen, Yvonne, I've got to talk to you. Put on a bath-robe or something. It's an emergency."

"What's the matter?"

"Open the door, for God's sakes."

From his chair Truston spoke up. "Open the door for him."

Mrs. Melli opened the door. Joseph walked in. His face was red, swollen almost; he looked as though he had been crying. He was holding his left arm next to his body.

"What's the matter? Are you O.K.? You look like you got hurt."

"Can't we go talk privately?"

190

"This is Mr. Clapp, it's all right. He's from one of the committees. He's interviewing me. Mrs. Melli isn't going to bother you. This is my brother Joseph." Yvonne turned as if to present him to Truston. Joseph sat down on the bed.

"Did you hurt your arm? What happened, did you get into a fight?" Mr. Clapp from the committee was taking over.

"Now, Mr. Clapp," Mrs. Melli recovered, "let Miss Rhode Island here deal with this."

"I'm concerned about the boy."

"Thanks," Joseph said. He seemed to be less flushed now. But his arm was still red; it seemed swollen. Suddenly he took his hand away from it. He jabbed it forward, it was distended. He held it out so Yvonne could see.

He had got a tattoo.

Big, all over his arm.

Gross.

There it was, almost wiggling.

The ink, lipstick red.

"That's just disgusting." Yvonne choked on the words. She had to keep staring at it.

At her.

The hips, the breasts, naked. The Y of the belly and the thighs, bright red. Was there still blood on it?

"I just got it." Joseph let his arm fall. "This one too." On his lower arm there was another tattoo: an anchor. "Now I wish I didn't."

"They don't ever come off." Was Yvonne crying? Her brother, making Miss Rhode Island upset. "What made you do something stupid like that? What's the matter with you?" A shriek, hysterical, not a Wellesley girl's

191

voice, not the voice of Miss Rhode Island. Joseph looked away from her; he looked toward Truston. For help maybe.

Yvonne went over to Joseph, she put her hands on his shoulders, over his swollen arm, she shook him. "Why did you do that? Why did you do it?"

She slapped him.

"Hey, take it easy." Truston stood up.

"You keep out of it, Truston." The first time she had ever shouted at him. Like Miss Woonsocket, a mill girl.

"Perhaps you ought to leave now, Mr. Clapp." Mrs. Melli held out her hand in invitation. A plea. "Mr. Clapp, I'll telephone you after things calm down."

"Is that your friend Truston?" Joseph started to laugh. "My God, I never figured I'd meet you." He went over to Truston to shake hands.

Lightly Truston brushed his fingertips over the tattoo. "You're marked for life, fella," he said. "Those things never come off once they're on."

"Who told you I've got a friend named Truston?" Yvonne's voice was back to normal. Subnormal, actually. It was very quiet. "Who said anything to you?"

"I just happened to know, that's all." With his hand Joseph covered up the tattoo again.

"Who told you? Who talked to you about it?"

Truston looked just as guilty as Joseph did.

"It was Julie, it was that bitch Julie. Get out of here." Yvonne reached for the chair she had been sitting on earlier, she held on to its back. Was she going to lift it up? Miss Rhode Island the lion tamer, the huntress, the scourge of the wild boar, Bella Furiosa, watch her act. Now doesn't she look beautiful? Now don't you wish you had hold of her? That's the way you like them, when they get mad, when they start to cry out, you can feel it inside them, that's when you want to grab them most. The chair was against her breasts—oh, couldn't you just reach for them, was she going to throw the chair? Oh, wouldn't you love to catch it. Throw it yourself and start pushing back at her! Those little feet in the high-heeled shoes. Let her kick! Wouldn't you want to grab hold while she was kicking? Miss Maine, I want to Bangor! Miss Mass., feel that ass! Who wants to waste time with other girls, wouldn't you rather have this one, let her shout all she wants. The more she shouts, the more she pushes. Jesus, isn't she something! Miss R.I., U. R. O.K. This one ought to be Miss America. Miss Ore., what a whore! Oh, Miss Kentuck, come on, let's. Let's do it! You're the one that's got the swing for it. Look at those tits. Best breast. Ass class. Tit, slit. Miss Pussy America, I got you now.

"Get out! Get out of here! Get out of here, both of you!" Yvonne let go of the chair, it tipped over, it fell onto the floor, she kicked it out of her way, she was crying, she turned around away from them. "Get out of here!" She ran into the bathroom and pushed the door shut. She locked it, she turned on the water loud, both faucets to drown out the sound of her crying. She flushed, she turned on the bathtub water too. All she could hear was the sound of water crashing, she didn't know if they were still there, she couldn't hear the door closing, she couldn't hear voices, only the water. Also the sound of knocking.

"They're gone now."

It was Mrs. Melli.

"Open the door, Yvonne, they went away."

Mrs. Melli knocked again on the bathroom door.

"Shut off the water."

"Are they gone?"

"They're gone."

"Both of them?"

"Both gone."

Yvonne opened the door.

"Come here, baby." Mrs. Melli held out her arms. "That was awful, baby."

"They're both such pigs." Yvonne let Mrs. Melli put her arms around her. She sat down on a chair. Mrs. Melli's breasts—Yvonne's head was on them.

"I always told you about him." Mrs. Melli never surrendered. "Tattoos aren't so bad. A lot of them get tattoos. My husband even got a tattoo. The same thing, the naked lady."

"But he got it before he knew you."

"Don't keep crying now, Yvonne, you got to stop crying. Your eyes are going to look like hell. Maybe you ought to lie down now. He got it only a couple of years ago, he thought it was going to cheer me up."

Yvonne got up and lay down on the bed. Mrs. Melli went over to her, she took off Yvonne's high-heeled shoes.

"Why would he think you'd like it?"

"That's better now, no crying. That's the way. He got it put on his behind. He wanted to show me he was going to stick by me even though I had my operation." Mrs. Melli sat down on Yvonne's bed. "Because I had my mastectomy."

"You had a mastectomy?" Yvonne turned over and hid her face in the pillow.

Was she kidding? Could you forget something like that?

"You didn't know that? Two years ago, I thought I told you."

194

"I'm sorry. I'm terribly sorry." Yvonne was crying again.

"You mean you didn't know? I thought I told you, cut that crying."

"If I knew, I forgot."

"Look at me!" Yvonne didn't turn around. "No, lift your face, look at me, stop crying now. You're going to ruin your eyes. Some of the girls cry every time, the judges can see it the next day. Look at me."

"I can't tell which one."

"The left one." Mrs. Melli leaned forward. The demonstration. "The left, see, you still can't tell. It don't even have a seam, it's the best kind, it moves when you move, that's how they advertise. It won't ever happen to you." Mrs. Melli crossed herself. "Jesus God, I hope not. But if it does, I got the name of the place. You can't get them in Providence, you have to go to Boston. It's expensive. Blue Cross don't pay for it, Major Medical pays, you might as well get the best."

"I don't want to know."

More screaming.

"Why did you have to tell me?"

"You got to cut out that shouting." Mrs. Melli got up off the bed. "It's not good for you."

Wrong.

Mrs. Melli doesn't know everything.

Once, in the 1930s, a winner screamed the day before the final judging.

One time during the Korean War, the winner screamed, she cried the entire night through. In this same hotel.

Screaming calls them forth.

195

Mrs. Melli wasn't listening. Her hands, over her ears, block out the sound.

But in the heavens, Victoria, Pulchritudo, they are listening.

None of the other girls is screaming.

XIII

Iowa was a Tridelt. Tennessee was Kappa Kappa Gamma, so was Montana; oh, how they fell into each other's arms when they met. Tennessee did acrobatic dancing, Montana did too. "Maybe we can be a team, maybe we can go on the nightclub circuit: the Kappa Kappa Misses."

Miss Maryland, the only black. Her song, "Un bel di," by Giacomo Puccini. There was one other opera, plus three semi-classical.

How stupid of Minnesota to sing "In the Blue Canadian Rockies"! Let her enter Miss Canada with that one.

Miss Arkansas, she was the one with the baton twirling. Of course, there had to be one. But the surprise of it was this: She was good, it was fun to watch. Why joke about it? It was better than a no-good rendition of a fine talent.

But there was one very gifted girl there, a flutist. She played a piece entitled *Syrinx*, by Claude Debussy. It lasted more than three minutes, but she was good enough to hold them for the extra time. She had worked in a movie, the Walt Disney Studio Symphony. You could feel the music in your breasts. She was from Oregon.

She was so good Yvonne felt safe going over to her afterward. "How did you get into this?"

197

Oregon examined her carefully for a minute. She had long honey-blond hair, and a composed middle-class look to her face. "My mother got after me. It was calculated. I'm not here for pretty, I'm here to get out of the Disney studio. It's hard for flutists to get real work."

"It was beautiful." Oregon didn't care about winning.

"It's tough to get a flute job. There's no jobs except playing junk. You know what I have to do at Disney, sit all day playing trills behind a chipmunk. You go to Wellesley. What are you doing here?"

"I don't know what I'm doing here." She was prettier than Miss Oregon, that's what she was doing here. "All I play is the piano, but I'm not good at it, I picked ice skating for a talent. I don't give a damn about that, though." My only preoccupation is: My Beauty. "I'm aiming to be a Latin professor. I love Latin poetry. I get embarrassed about it, it sounds cuckoo. Nobody else cares about it. Nobody's said the words for so long; there's nobody there but me and these gods and goddesses, some trees in Italy. It's like a little house I'm building, no one's ever seen it but me, not even the poet."

"I understand it," Miss Oregon said. "It keeps boys out."

But Yvonne had liked boys before she became Miss Rhode Island. She liked Poulos. Didn't she like Poulos?

Still, whenever they could, they sat next to each other.

Actually, some of the Misses weren't that bad. There was nobody in New England, the South was a loss, all those girls cared about was winning, but there were some nice Western girls: Oregon; Utah, a short intent ballet dancer; Nebraska, a piano player.

But most were not nice.

198

"What's it like coming from such a teeny state like Rhode Island?" The question was from Miss Arizona.

"Cozy."

Another question: Did popularity with the other girls help win the contest? If so, was it worth it?

Another question: If Truston walked into the Convention Hall, with all of them standing around on the stage rehearsing the TV show, waiting while the hired professionals, the real singers, the real dancers—they were called the talent—moved from downstage to upstage and back over the tape marks that wouldn't show on TV, would Truston choose her? Poulos was out there somewhere in one of the seats of the enormous hall watching her now. Joseph was out there too, beside him. Another question: Was Truston there too? Mrs. Melli said he had gone home. He had promised. " 'I'll watch it on TV.' Those were his very words."

Another question: Was Mrs. Melli telling the truth?

Girls over twenty to the right. Girls under twenty to the left.

Girls from east of the Mississippi on this side, from the west on that side. Miss Louisiana is from Baton Rouge, but she goes with the wests.

No, the blondes in the front. All others in back.

Girls over and under 5'5". Anything under 36C in the back row.

All the girls in cool-color swimsuits—blue tones, greens—on this side. Hot colors—red, yellow, like that —into the pool. Quick now, hop to it, splash.

The tallest girl is not Texas or Alaska. The shortest girl is not Rhode Island. Nor is Rhode Island the one with the smallest bust.

All the girls from New England over here for the picture. Manchester *Union Leader,* Worcester *Telegram,* Waterbury *Republican, The Berkshire Eagle.*

"I've been looking for you. How's your arm? You all healed up?" It was Miss Texas. She looked just like the picture enclosed in the letter she sent when Yvonne had broken her arm; but now she was blown up, a little puffy. (As soon as she had won the Miss Rhode Island contest, Yvonne had plotted out her period. Thank God! Two weeks after Labor Day, after the pageant was over.) Miss Texas—the moon wasn't with her. According to talk, it was California everyone had to watch out for.

Yvonne's strongest grip, shaking Texas's hand. "I'm fine," she said. "And how are you?" To her dismay, the words came out with a mock Southern accent. "I bet you'd like to meet some of the other girls from New England, there's Miss New Hampshire." A Texan would be interested in a girl who was planning to be a veterinarian. And Miss New Hampshire would speak in a scanty New England way, reinforcement.

"You call me Texas. Could I call you Rhody?"

"Don't you dare."

Miss Texas was tall, she leaned forward excitedly, too close to Yvonne. A lesbian? Her mouth was open. Yvonne could see that her makeup needed smoothing, but only on one cheek. "And what'll happen if I do?"

"I'll work out something." Miss New Hampshire was only a few feet away.

"Watch out." Miss Texas looked very happy. "I'll rassle you down."

"This is Miss New Hampshire. We're almost neighbors. You ought to meet Texas."

Miss Texas put her arm around Yvonne and squeezed her shoulder. "You're real cute. I didn't think a gal from New England could be cute like that."

Miss New Hampshire had a valid complaint. "I only have five hundred dollars for wardrobe. Some of the girls from the South get a lot more. They get cosmetic money. I have to buy cosmetics out of my five hundred. Bathing suit, shoes, gown, everything. Could you buy a complete wardrobe for five hundred dollars? I couldn't. My uncle had to lend me some money. In the South, they get falls, Miss America in a wig! That's crazy. If they pick me, they got me."

Away from Texas. Away from New Hampshire.

"I got a thousand dollars' worth of chips." Miss Nevada was six feet tall. She weighed 144 pounds. "And I played up to forty-three hundred, but then I started losing. So I left with four fifty. Then I went back another time and brought it up to sixteen hundred. I think they tilted it. The man at the table liked me."

"If they caught Miss Alabama gambling, they'd knock my crown off."

"Isn't that marvelous!" Miss Michigan. They all wore neat little pins. Names and addresses. "This nation is so varied, there can be room for different outlooks, regardless of race or creed."

"Alabama is unsophisticated, I have to admit." Miss Alabama was very blond.

Next to her, Miss Oregon hardly looked blond at all.

"I think the whole country's unsophisticated," she said.

"Take it easy, don't dump on Maine." An unsophisticated remark.

But of course Miss Maine wouldn't win. No girl from New England ever won.

ROMAN SPA it said in Gothic lettering over the door. LADIES ONLY. A rose twined around the O in ONLY.

Beside the door was a cardboard sign lettered with a pink Magic Marker: "Reserved for Miss America Contestants Only, Today."

Each girl had a little closet of her own just to hang her clothes in. "Hi." Miss Texas brushed against Yvonne. "You going for the facial first or the sauna? Whyn't you come sit in the sauna with me?"

"I never had a facial before."

"I'm tired of facials. I had a facial every week. My committee sponsors it. Didn't your committee even give you facials?"

"So, I have to cram all my facial into today."

"I'll have a facial too." Miss Oregon's committee paid for facials, but only once a month. They also paid for a winter vacation in the Bahamas, so she could keep her tan. They gave $1500 for wardrobe. Free cosmetics, her choice. Ownership, not just use, of a car. And one performance with the Portland Symphony, with her as soloist. Well reviewed too.

When they handed out white sheets to each girl, Oregon whispered, "I bet Alabama feels right at home in these."

Yvonne didn't say anything.

"K.K.K." Oregon explained it.

She sat on Yvonne's left. On Yvonne's right, Nevada. Beyond Nevada, Alabama. Black masks, mud, on all of them. Miss Africa. "Don't talk now," the beautician, attractive herself, a blonde, said. "You'll crack." White towels were twisted around their hair, like turbans. A row of them, votive idols, black and white.

The black mask, you yourself have worn it, more than once. You have wrapped yourself in the white sheet. Ceremoniously, you have rolled the white turban around your head, you have held your face still. You have walked under the archway. You have sweated. But were you allowed to approach them?

If you have been allowed, then you have been chosen. I have not been.

Are you on this side? Or are you on that?

Yvonne fell asleep.

When she awoke, she had cracked.

Had she spoken? She had heard sounds. Was it she who had made them? Whose voice? "You're going to win, you look terrific, you got more class than they do." Had she already finished Swimsuit and been judged? Or was Swimsuit coming up?

The mask was off. There was a hot damp cloth on her face. A Southern voice was saying, "Deep pores."

"Pores." She could hear Oregon speaking, with her sturdy Rs. "Pores to rhyme with whores."

"You girls are really something." Alabama didn't sound shocked.

"I pronounce it po-uh too," Yvonne said, "and ho-uh."

"In Nevada we have legal whorehouses."

"It's not that different from a beauty contest." Miss Oregon's voice. Was she that lib?

"That's disgusting. Why go into a contest if you don't respect it? You don't respect yourself then. They don't feel that way in Alabama. You don't feel that way, Rhody, do you?"

"A little bit. Where does this mud come from?" Yvonne rubbed her cheek.

"It's mineralized. I don't know." Miss Alabama still had a little mud on her chin.

"I bet it's from New Jersey. Is she around here, Miss New Jersey? She got her mud all over us."

"My God, I've been using Alabama mud all year and

now I'm switching. It could be bad for the complexion. Even in Swimsuit they look at complexion." Alabama wiggled around in her chair looking for a mirror. "It might be different minerals. I'll check with the doctor. I hope it's O.K."

"What doctor?"

"In my retinue. Don't you have a doctor? My committee has a doctor in attendance for me."

"I don't have a doctor. I don't have facials. This is my first facial and now it's New Jersey mud and it's going to ruin my chances." Was Yvonne really kidding?

"Don't worry, honey, it will be all right." Was Miss Alabama really sincere?

The deep cleanser, the cream scrub, the steam moisturizer, were they enough to get the mud out?

In the sauna, the steam was New Jersey steam, the shower was New Jersey water. The North screamed and the South screamed. "Oh, it's too cold." Yvonne chose the bubble bath instead.

"I don't like bubbles, you made a big mistake," Miss Alabama said to her. "Bubbles are not good for the skin. It's like detergent."

"I haven't put as much thought into it as you have."

"Oh, you got to. It says so in the beauty books, not in the magazines, because they need ads from, you know, the bubble industry. Besides, didn't your committee tell you? Your chaperone?"

"We don't take it so seriously in Rhode Island."

"That's why the Southern girls win all the time." Miss Alabama looked like this year's winner right now. In two hours, after the hairdresser, it would be time for Swimsuit. Before dinner, fortunately. No bad little bulges.

"You have to take it seriously. Why go? You didn't really mean that about the prostitute?"

"Maybe I didn't."

Ay, Kirby. Ay, Fino. The finalists. Do you hear the ripping open of the envelopes, the harsh, hissing sound as if the earth itself is being ripped open. Poulos, Joseph, down there in the audience among the Americans, you will hear it announced. Are you among the immortals now?

Ten are taken, forty are discarded, spit out like seeds that will never sprout.

Here is where the career of Miss Rhode Island ends.

The man stands holding his little microphone, smiling.

Ay, Truston, time is passing by. Will your wife turn off the TV or will she turn it louder? Vee, vee. Louder.

Miss Alabama, Sherry Lee Fitcomb of Birmingham.

The roar of Alabamans begins. A girl's squeal, a shriek, the other forty-nine. Have they won too or have they lost? This shriek, mourning or triumph?

Miss Arizona, Suzanne Burdick of Yuma.

Miss California, Purlene McDonald of Bakersfield.

Miss Connecticut, Carol Fuller of Woodbury.

This shriek, this stamping of feet, this roaring, complete.

Thus New England is served. Yvonne is finished. Scat! Now we know it: Who is more beautiful.

"Oh, no!" The voice of Charlotte Arnold of the Rhode Island Arnolds. Do you hear it surging over the audience, through the TV screen? Truston heard it, perhaps he said it. Mrs. Melli, now you know what you have always known: The answer is no.

As Miss Connecticut scampers up to join the winners standing in a line in their long gowns, Yvonne, unthinkingly, takes a step backward; she is not lined up with the others. Is she withdrawing? The line is ragged, all the choreography wasted. Can they see the lapse on TV? It is to weep. It is to stand there with the other losers listening. Florida, Hawaii, Minnesota. It is to sink gracefully into the past, the morning glory closing. It is to curse the goddess, to lie upon the beach mute among stones, feeling the beating of the waves.

Michigan, Nebraska, Nevada, Oregon. Now Truston is truly lost, now Kirby. Now the battle has ended, South Kingstown has won, North Kingstown has lost. Now the football season is over, now the trophy has gone, there, away, to the other town. Now the brother has vanished, now Doucette, now Arnold; they have faded into the earth. It is finished.

Miss Rhode Island, Yvonne Doucette of North Kingstown.

Vee.

Outside, across the boardwalk, ocean roaring.

Joseph jumping.

Imagine, two finalists from New England! That must be a first.

It takes pushing, the soft hands of the losers, Massachusetts, Pennsylvania, Iowa, their long fingers, even their nails, digging into Yvonne's bare shoulders, to move her out of the line of the losers into the line of the winners.

The winners? Ten finalists.

These. Plus Texas.

Eliminated: all the border states. The entire Louisiana Purchase except for Nebraska. Alaska, Hawaii, out. The old Confederacy east of the Mississippi, out, except for Alabama. The old Northwest Territory, out, except for Michigan. Territories acquired in the Mexican War—Arizona, California, Nevada—a powerful threat, especially counting Texas. The thirteen original colonies, all out, almost, including their ancillary territories—Maine, once part of Massachusetts; Vermont, once disputed between New York and New Hampshire. Only two of the original thirteen surviving: Miss Connecticut—it was her singing that did it; and don't forget her, everybody's heroine, Yvonne Miss Rhode Island Doucette.

From the St. Jean Baptiste Union of Woonsocket, a loud cheer, and in French. Elle est belle, elle est belle, Miss Rhode Island, elle est belle. Yvonne, standing up in line with the other finalists, holding her bouquet of red roses—thank God! it keeps the hands from fidgeting—could see them down there on the right side of the auditorium (was it an omen?) cheering, two rows of them; could see people turning around to see who was shouting in a foreign language, a nonsense cheer: Elle est belle. Behind them some losers, unsmiling, waved a placard that said, forlornly, "Go, go, go, Indiana." They should save it for the football season, only a few weeks away.

Walk down the runway. Finalists and losers. Last chance. Take your bow. All the dark people out there. Out of lightness they came and now they are in darkness, looking up at the light shining out from between the legs, annuit coeptis, the rays.

A hundred breasts, a hundred eyes, a hundred arms lined up waving. Miss Michigan is a Syrian girl named Alice Hajim. She does a belly dance. It brings attention to Michigan; it brings to the notice of the public the fact that Arab-Americans form an important and growing part of our nation. E pluribus unum, but she can't win. No Arab can be chosen Miss America.

Connecticut has a phenomenal talent. A simple song, "Melancholy Baby," but she has a beautiful voice and she knows how to use it, she sounds professional. When she went onstage, she said to Yvonne, "Now you're going to hear it," and when she came off, all the girls applauded, sincerely. Even the judges applauded.

"I'm going to make it my profession," after she finished singing. "There's no question about it. I've been studying five years. There's a jazz pianist from New York, he has a summer place up in my town and he likes to work with me and he's going to get me a job."

No lie, this one's for real, not another Madam Butterfly. Don't think you won't be seeing her starring on TV someday.

"My real talent is as a horsewoman. I have performed with the All-Girl Chariot Race at the Texas State Fair and as a solo rider at the Llano County Fair in Texas. But because we can't get horses into the pageant arena here, I will do acrobatic dancing to the tune of 'The Eyes of Texas Are upon You.' " Mostly walking on hands, a one-hand stand. Twisting, this way and that.

Miss Dixie: a Frisbee juggle. Miss Megalopolis: roller skating. Miss San Andreas Fault: a humorous chalk-talk, "What I Didn't Do Last Summer." Miss North Slope: an imitation of a bulldozer.

And Miss Rhode Island: Frozen music. Grace on Ice.

"Break a leg!" nine girls called out to Yvonne as she skated out onto the ice.

That was the customary way they wished girls luck here.

Water for the ice had come from a reservoir in the New

208

Jersey pinewoods. The skating costume had been made in South Carolina, in a mill, with cloth woven in North Carolina. Rayon thread spun in Pennsylvania, from Texas oil. The skates: leather hide from Nebraska, steel blades from Minnesota. Holding Yvonne's hair, a plastic barrette made in New York.

The musicians, playing the *Water Music* by George Handel, born in six different states. They came in two colors, black and white.

It was fast music. The great trick: whirling while lowering the body to do a sit spin, arms outstretched. The second great trick: whirling with one leg extended, then lowering the body backward. Was there a talent scout from the Ice Capades in the hall?

Ellie Donovan from Woonsocket has a crooked tooth. She is small-busted. Her hips are too wide. She doesn't go out on enough dates, but her friend Sue Drinan fixes her up. She works in the bakery on Providence Street on Saturdays, her swift fingers folding the cardboard cake box, breaking off the string, tying the bow.

Mary Ann Facelli slouches when she walks. Her lips are too thick, her complexion isn't good.

Amy Lavalette is skinny, she has dark hair on her arms. She is learning stenotyping so she can become a court reporter.

Donna Wilk has to let boys feel her up in order to get a date. Even in the summertime, her face is pale. Her hair always looks tangled.

Yvonne went lower on one leg, she whirled around, she kept her smile steady.

Linda Paro forgot her part in the Christmas play, someone else had to cover up for her and make something up.

209

The music surged, Yvonne rose up like the swan taking wing, the great gull with wings spread. Audubon would have painted her, if he had seen.

Sandy Wallach cries whenever she gets her period.

Laurel Monaghan slapped a boy once just because he kissed her. She's crazy, like in the funny papers.

Yvonne, inside, began humming soundlessly along with the music. It was going wonderfully.

Phyllis Tetreault fell down in the playground and broke her leg. She had been climbing the jungle gym. Imagine, a college girl like that.

Angie Cappagola was in a motorcycle crash. Her spine is broken. She's lucky she's alive. They were going around on Route 1 near Narragansett in the fog and it skidded.

Into another whirl. The right foot first, giving the push, and then the left. Yvonne started going faster and faster. Her foot pointed, it went up, she raised it poised beside the other leg; she whirled around; there she goes, as fast as Sonja Henie, as fast as Tenley Albright, as fast as any Russian or any Czechoslovakian you see on the Wide Wide World of Sports, or fast as the Ice Capettes, the Folliettes, the Ice Chips, as fast as God could make her go, around and around. Would she go into a time warp? Would she spin so fast she just turned wavy and disappeared? Watch her go! Look now, this is your last chance. She's going too fast to see, there she goes into the invisible. The Miss Americas have never seen anything like it, the Ice Capades, the Olympics; it's the fastest spin in ice-skating history. Whirl! Whirl! Into the land of the ice princess, the snow queen, our little Yvonne, it's dangerous, hold your breath, she might never come out of it alive, right before our eyes, she might never come back, just like a snowflake, taken up by the whirlwind.

Miss Tornado. Miss Blizzard. Don't look, shut your eyes, it shouldn't be seen, there's something dangerous about it, even for the people watching; you could be swept up in it too, up around and around; like the whirling dervishes, caught up around herself! Is she slowing down?

Kathy Cobb ran away from home. One day she was there, the next day she was gone; she just disappeared.

Patsy Walker turned eighteen, she just sat in her room and wouldn't go out of the house. She said she was all right, but nobody could come near her. They just brought her her meals. The only time she leaves the room is to go into the bathroom.

Yvonne slowly raised her arms. They were whirling around too.

A high wail! A whine! Is it the sound of the blades? A siren? Harsh. Quick, cover your ears, you could go mad.

Somewhere in that blur is Yvonne Doucette of Pleasant Street, Wickford, North Kingstown, Rhode Island.

Like the earth spinning, she goes around and around, creating time.

Can you hear the applause start? First a few hands clapping, Rhode Island hands, then the entire audience. They shout, they thunder. Even in the houses, in California, in Maine, the TV watchers far away, they are applauding too.

It isn't beauty alone that makes you Miss America. Take a look carefully when you see her picture the next morning in the Sunday paper. That's exactly what you say when you see Miss America: She isn't that pretty.

It's a gift, talent, turn their heads. The goddess Pulchritudo sits among the Fates. As they spin, turning the thread around and around swiftly with their nimble fingers, swiftly Yvonne turns too, her blades flashing. Watch out for the sharpness, do not cut the thread.

211

Great care must be taken.

Swiftness is one thing.

Care is another.

Turning and turning, the loud applause, a roar. It makes space disappear.

Is she still here among the mortals, or has she whirled away to become one of *them?*

The competition is over, the time has come to an end, everyone else has lost. I have lost, you have lost, and your girlfriend, she is a loser too, admit it.

I remember how I felt the day I put my arm around Janet, I was wearing my football jacket—purple and white—I had my letter, not bad; but always there was this: It's only Janet, it is not Yvonne.

Not that you can't be satisfied, not that you can't go through life and come out the other side to that place where even the goddess does not dare to go, "the region of shadows and of sleep and of drowsy night"; there the faces are gone, the eyes are gone; that place where Helen dwells, that place of the first Miss America, the place of the thousand Arnolds, the thousand Doucettes. Enjoy it now—only Janet. Careful, you could lose even her.

I am losing.

Is it her beauty that has destroyed me? Or is it my ugliness? Do I have to admit it? The place where the thighs widen; the look on the face, sorrow. Judging, will I be judged?

Oh, it's Yvonne, it is her beauty! I lower my head, I hide, from her pitiless face. It's only when I hear the voice say it—"The Winner!"—only when I hear the metallic smiling voice of the master of ceremonies, only when I see him gray on the television screen saying it out loud: "The Winner, this year's winner, there she is, the new Miss America, Suzanne Burdick, Miss Arizona," only then do I dare look up at her, sweet Yvonne.

Perhaps, even so, she is the prettier one.

On the white sheets, Yvonne's thrashing legs. Now Truston has been killed, his breath has stopped. Truston, a loser.

A paradox: He would have lost, even more, if she had won.

Oh, it isn't fair. The beautiful nose, stuffed up. Oh, it isn't fair. The beautiful eyes, red. Oh, it isn't fair. The legs hitting the bed. The fist, hitting once, hitting again. Oh God, it isn't fair.

Do you remember when you lay on the bed, crying like this?

Oh Christ, it isn't fair. Rocking back and forth, the body twisted, the hair wet, hanging in front of the eyes, oh God, it isn't fair.

Is Joseph fair, Nelda Mack? Oh God, it isn't fair.

Mrs. Melli of the one breast, oh God, it isn't fair. The forehead hitting the bed, the head bowed, a knife, a small knife, the point of a small knife, if she had one there with her on the bed in Atlantic City after the judging, a knife against the breast, here, this, the left, oh God, it isn't fair. Are you the sort of person who destroys what beauty is remaining? Oh God, it isn't fair. Mrs. Melli might come back into the room. The crying a series of coughs. How soundproof is the room? How soundproof is your room, the house, the air?

Outside the hotel room, the waves—they are all different, but they all look alike—end their histories by disappearing into the sands of the beach.

Rejoice, Marilyn, rejoice!

Fino, you are revenged!

Joseph, now you cannot have her.

213

Truston: a husk.

Rejoice, Julie! Reader, rejoice!

God, it isn't fair.

The phone call from Truston. It didn't come.

What is worse? Having Julie as a roommate when you might be Miss America, or having her there staring at you in Pomeroy Hall when you never will be Miss America?

Joseph, now you are free to grow up. The great trial is over, as over as it will ever be.

Already the new apples are golden, hanging on their branches.

This time, returning from Atlantic City, the underwear is not neatly folded in the suitcase. "I've never seen a girl pack like you." Mrs. Melli put her arms around Yvonne. "I've never seen a girl take it so hard. Rhode Island always loses, it's not so bad. Do you want me to pack for you?"

Yvonne's answer: a nod. She lay down on the bed and took one of Mrs. Melli's cigarettes and lit it. Now she was a smoker.

Out of the suitcase Mrs. Melli scooped handfuls of dirty laundry, bras that had clasped those sweetly formed breasts, underpants—some lace, some silken—all of them had embraced Miss Rhode Island's hips, they had brushed along her thighs, they had rubbed against her blond belly. Each one was carefully folded, laid down gently in the suitcase next to the neatly rolled panty hose, next to the dresses that had rustled around Yvonne's knees, the tiny golden combs that had run through her hair.

"Next time," Mrs. Melli said, as if there actually was going to be a next time, "I guess we're going to have to play it a little different."